LETHAL WEAPON

The noise of a branch breaking drew Nancy's gaze into the shrubbery. Moonlight gleamed on a metallic object. Small branches quivered.

There's somebody in there! Nancy thought. Somebody who might want to hurt George and Ragnar.

Suddenly a gloved fist rose above the bushes. Nancy recognized the long, slender object in its grasp. A javelin!

"Look out!" Nancy screamed. She was in motion even as she cried out. She made a diving leap toward the astounded couple.

Too late! The javelin cut through the air, right on target for Ragnar and George . . .

IN THE ALL-NEW SUPERMYSTERY
STARRING NANCY DREW
AND THE HARDY BOYS

Nancy Drew & Hardy Boys SuperMysteries

DOUBLE CROSSING
A CRIME FOR CHRISTMAS
SHOCK WAVES
DANGEROUS GAMES

Available from ARCHWAY Paperbacks

DANGEROUS GAMES

Carolyn Keene

AN ARCHWAY PAPERBACK
Published by POCKET BOOKS
New York London Toronto Sydney Tokyo

This book is a work of fiction. Names, characters, places and incidents are either the product of the author's imagination or are used fictitiously. Any resemblance to actual events or locales or persons, living or dead, is entirely coincidental.

AN ARCHWAY PAPERBACK *Original*

An Archway Paperback published by
POCKET BOOKS, a division of Simon & Schuster Inc.
1230 Avenue of the Americas, New York, NY 10020

Produced by Mega-Books of New York, Inc.

ISBN: 0-671-64920-5

First Archway Paperback printing August 1989

10 9 8 7 6 5 4 3 2 1

Printed in the U.S.A.

IL 7+

Chapter One

I'M JUST GLAD a new mall doesn't open every day," George Fayne groaned as she helped her cousin Bess Marvin with her packages.

"You said it," Nancy Drew agreed, laughing. She was holding the back door to her house open for Bess, whose arms were piled high with still more bags.

George set the boxes down on the Drews' kitchen table and ran her hands through her short, dark hair. "What did you do anyway, Bess, buy out Eastman's?" she asked.

Bess's blue eyes sparkled as she tossed back her long, blond hair. "I just thought I'd pick up a few things."

"A few?" George echoed.

Nancy smiled. The three of them had just spent a hectic July afternoon at the brand-new Westlake Mall. Bess could be a demon when it came to shopping.

"You and Nancy managed to buy a few things, too," Bess said. "Like that sea green cashmere sweater that the saleswoman said went so well with your reddish blond hair and blue eyes, Nancy."

"Those salespeople sure can flatter a girl," Nancy said. "Look, while you two are fighting it out over who spent more, I'm going to check the answering machine. Be right back."

Beep! "Nancy—" It was her boyfriend, Ned Nickerson. Hearing his voice always sent a warm flutter through her. "There's some trouble out here. The kind only you can solve. It could be a matter of life and death for a certain someone. Call me for details." He left a number where he could be reached.

Nancy's curiosity was aroused. Ned wouldn't call asking for help all the way from California if it weren't important. During the year, Ned was a student at Emerson College, but he worked summers for an insurance company. This year, his firm had stationed him in California at the International Championship Games at Santa Teresa to process competitors' insurance applications.

Nancy switched off the machine and dialed Ned's office number in California.

Ned's office manager came on the line. Ned wasn't there, but he had left instructions about the arrangements he had made for her and Bess and George.

After calling the airline, Nancy hurried downstairs. She found Bess and George at the kitchen table, drinking sodas.

"What's up, Nan?" George asked.

"Ned called. He's stumbled over a mystery. What do you guys say to a trip to Santa Teresa, California?"

"What's in Santa Teresa?" Bess asked, taking a sip of her soda.

"Only the International Championship Games, starring world-class track-and-field and swimming athletes." George's brown eyes lit up. "It's a very prestigious competition—the best are invited to attend."

"I think I saw all those incredible hunks on 'Cavalcade of Sports.'" Bess's eyelashes fluttered. "Gorgeous guys with wide, wide shoulders. And I've got the new things to wear. When do we leave?"

"Typical," George said with a groan.

Nancy grinned. "As soon as you pack. We fly out now and spend the night at an airport motel in Los Angeles—then tomorrow, on to the games."

* * *

The next morning Nancy was settled back in the airport limo's plush seat. Beside her sat Bess and George, eagerly discussing the upcoming Games, which were to start in three days. The athletes were just arriving now.

Peering out the tinted window, Nancy watched the wheatgrass-covered hills drift by. Beyond them, the taller, greener Tularosa Mountains challenged a cloudless azure sky.

Santa Teresa was at least a hundred miles north of Los Angeles. Even with the eight-lane Camino freeway, the traffic made it a two-hour drive from L.A.

George spent most of the drive filling them in on the Games. Sports were her first love, and she knew every American contestant's background by heart.

"Everyone's counting on Dave Gillespie to take the gold in the decathlon," George said. "He's been smashing records since he started competing two years ago. Last year he topped Malinovsky's discus record."

Bess looked slightly confused. "You throw a discus in a decathlon?"

"A decathlon isn't a single event, Bess," Nancy explained. "It's ten, one after the other. The competition shows who's the best all-around athlete."

"And those are killer events," George added. "You have to do the whole thing in only two days. Five events each day."

"Wow!" Bess let out a low whistle.

George went on. "You know," she said, "some classic records have been set at decathlons. No one had ever beaten the magic three hundred in the javelin until Jim Overton came along."

"What's the magic three hundred?" Nancy asked.

"No one had ever been able to throw a javelin three hundred feet," George explained. "Then, twelve years ago, Overton put his javelin right at three-oh-oh."

"That's all very interesting, George," Bess said, faking a yawn. "I can see why you're so fascinated by this case."

Glancing out the window, Nancy saw a highway sign pass overhead: Santa Teresa—Golden State University Next Exit.

The games were being held on the campus of Golden State. The limo whisked them up the university entrance, made a right turn, then another left, and they were headed up a long driveway, past sand-colored cinderblock buildings and well-trimmed shrubs. The top of what looked like a huge stadium stood out over a line of trees. In the distance, Nancy could see the thin blue line of the ocean.

The chauffeur dropped them off at the girls' dorm, Banning Hall, a modern four-story building with a fountain out front. After hauling their luggage inside, Nancy, Bess, and

George introduced themselves to the housing coordinator.

"Nancy Drew—right. I've put you girls in two-twelve. It's a triple," the woman said, handing Nancy three sets of keys. "You'll be sharing a floor with athletes. That's what I was told to do."

"Great," George said, as they headed for the elevator.

In their room, Nancy, Bess, and George changed into more comfortable T-shirts and shorts. Then they went back downstairs, and the coordinator gave them directions to the security office.

As they entered the nearby stadium, Nancy saw a group of U.S. runners jogging around the track, spurred on by their red-faced coach. Then she felt George's grip on her arm.

"Nancy, look!" George pointed out a tall, thin black man. He hefted a long aluminum pole, sprinted downfield, then hurled himself over a high crossbar with flawless precision.

"That's Joe Kanaga from Zaire! I've got to get his autograph." George turned to her cousin. "Bess, can I borrow your pen?"

"Huh?" Bess blinked as if coming out of a long sleep. "Did you say something, George?"

Wondering what had gotten Bess's rapt attention, Nancy looked to her right and saw a muscular young man in the middle of a white circle with a discus in his hand.

"Look at those shoulders!" Bess whispered.

With a cock of his arm, the man pivoted twice, and let fly. The discus hummed as it hurtled downfield.

Nancy led George and a dazed Bess toward the field house where the security offices were located. "I don't want to ruin anybody's good time," she said. "But Ned did sound pretty concerned. I bet we've got our work cut out for us."

"Don't worry, Nan. You can count on me," Bess said, her eyes glued to the athletes. She kept drifting away from Nancy and George.

"I just hope we get to meet some celebrities," George said, brushing strands of hair away from her face. "Hey, the wind sure does come up fast in California."

Nancy looked at the sky, wondering if they were in for a sudden shower. Out of the corner of her eye, she caught a glimpse of an athlete a hundred yards upfield, hurling a javelin.

A stiff gust brushed Nancy's face. She watched the javelin shudder in the wind. Its sharp-pointed nose suddenly dropped, veering to the left.

Nancy gasped. The speeding javelin was headed straight for Bess!

Chapter Two

"Bess! Watch out!"

Nancy dove and tackled her friend around the hips, forcing Bess to the ground.

The whir of displaced air filled Nancy's ears as the javelin passed no more than a foot over her head, pierced the nearby bleachers, and shuddered to a halt.

"You all right?" Nancy asked as she helped Bess to her feet.

"I think so." Bess took a deep breath. "What happened?"

Nancy was about to answer when Bess noticed the javelin. Her face turned white and she let out a little cry.

A crowd was forming around them as a chestnut-haired guy pushed up to them. He wiped the sweat from his forehead with the corner of his light gray sweatshirt.

"Are you okay?" he asked, first Nancy and then Bess. He took Bess by the shoulders. "I'm really sorry. I must have misjudged the wind speed."

The boy led Bess over to the bleachers, his arm around her waist. "Here, sit down. Let me call Doc Matthews."

"No, no, I'm really okay. Just a little shaken up. Look, why don't you get back to practice . . ." Bess's voice trailed off as she looked into the boy's eyes for the first time. Nancy watched her friend blush, take a deep breath, and force her eyes back to meet his green ones.

"Accidents do happen, don't they?" Bess said breathlessly.

"Well, now I know I can use more practice. I've always had trouble with my control." His lips turned in a tentative smile. "My name's Dave, Dave Gillespie."

"Bess Marvin," she said, flipping her hair back over her shoulder and reaching out to take Dave's extended hand.

Bess and Dave stood frozen, their hands clasped, as the crowd dispersed. A few guys were joking about how Dave managed to turn a near-fatal accident into an instant crush.

"Listen, Bess," Dave was saying, "let me make this up to you."

"It's okay, Dave. It wasn't your fault. It was probably the wind."

"I hate to break this up," Nancy said, strolling directly up to them. "But they *are* expecting us at the field house."

"We've got to go, Bess," George said pointedly.

"Are you staying here in town?" Dave asked as they were about to walk away. Bess nodded. "I'd like to take you to the pre-Games banquet tonight. All three of you," he quickly added.

"That'd be great! We're staying in Banning Hall," Bess said with a smile.

"It's a date." Dave grinned and pulled his javelin from the splintered bleacher. "See you at six in your dorm."

Nancy and George strode off to the exit with an unusually quiet and serious Bess tagging a few steps behind.

Minutes later Nancy was rapping on the open door of the field house.

Three men standing in the hallway turned to face them. One, a short, burly man with a bright pink complexion and unruly gray hair, asked if he could help them.

"Hi. I'm supposed to meet Ned Nickerson here. My name is Nancy Drew."

The gray-haired man beamed at Nancy and came forward to greet her.

"I'm glad you're here, Nancy. I'm Glen Hewitt, chief of Games security. You just missed Ned. His boss called him back to the office, but he said he'll call you later. Come on in."

Hewitt led Nancy, Bess, and George into a large office. The two men who had been standing in the hallway with Hewitt were already there.

"Gentlemen, this is the private detective Ned was telling us about—Nancy Drew," Hewitt said. He gestured to a fiftyish-year-old man with silvery hair. "Nancy, this is Dr. Clayton Matthews, our chief medical consultant. And this fellow is Jim Overton, one of the heads of the Games committee."

George blinked in recognition. "You're *the* Jim Overton, aren't you? The man who cracked the magic three hundred!"

Overton laughed politely. He was tall and rawboned, with thinning sandy hair and a firm chin. "I'm surprised anyone still remembers. It happened such a long time ago."

"Mr. Hewitt, these are my friends George Fayne and Bess Marvin," Nancy said.

"Glad to meet you," Hewitt said, shaking their hands. Suddenly his face screwed up, and he gave a tremendous sneeze. Reaching for a handkerchief, he smiled apologetically. "Sorry."

"Maybe you could tell us a little about

what's been going on," Nancy said. "We're still kind of in the dark."

Hewitt motioned for them to sit down. Overton and Matthews had already taken their seats. "Well, I was going to wait to start the briefing until the other detectives got here."

"Other detectives?" Nancy barely had time to ask Hewitt what he meant when a familiar male voice rang out.

"Hey, Drew, did you remember to bring your magnifying glass this time?"

"Joe Hardy!" Nancy turned at once. Her heart quickened at the sight of the dark-haired young man standing next to Joe. "Frank—"

"Hello, Nancy." Frank's arms opened in welcome. "It's great to see you again."

"Same here." Nancy embraced him, feeling her own smile widen. "It's been a while since Padre Island."

Frank's blond brother, Joe, tapped Nancy on the shoulder. "Don't I get one of those?"

"How could I forget you," Nancy said, giving him a hug. "What are you guys doing here, anyway?"

"That's just what I was going to ask," George said. "Hello, Frank. Hello, Joe."

"Hey, George," Frank said.

"What about me?" Bess asked in mock anger. She and the Hardys had always gotten along.

"You look great, Bess," Joe said with a smile.

Frank interrupted their reunion to answer Nancy's question. He nodded at the security chief. "Mr. Hewitt invited us. He's a friend of Dad's."

"Before I became a private investigator, I used to be the chief of detectives for the Santa Teresa PD," Hewitt told Nancy. "Fenton helped me out on a few cases. When I asked him to recommend a couple of good detectives, he told me his sons were the best."

Nancy watched Overton's face tense. "Glen," he said, "I don't doubt that these young people are competent. But I can't help wondering if this is really the right approach—"

"What do you mean?" Hewitt asked.

"Even though these games are small, the competition's the best and the committee's hoping for a big turnout," Overton answered. "We simply can't afford bad publicity." He stood up and began pacing Hewitt's office. "We can't let anyone know we have taken on extra security. That's the reason we didn't call the police in, remember?"

"Don't worry, Jim," Hewitt reassured him. "The Hardys, Ms. Drew, Ms. Fayne, and Ms. Marvin are all undercover."

Overton scowled. "I don't know. If the press

gets wind of our troubles, we could have a public relations disaster on our hands. And the more people involved, the more likely a leak to the media."

Frank Hardy cleared his throat. Nancy had observed him as he patiently listened to the conversation. But now he was getting antsy. "What exactly is the problem, Mr. Hewitt?" he asked.

Hewitt raised a questioning eyebrow at Overton, who nodded once—very slightly. Having been given a reluctant go-ahead, Glen Hewitt went to his desk, opened the center drawer, produced a wrinkled sheet of paper, and handed it to Frank.

Nancy crossed the room to read over Frank's shoulder. Cut-out words from a newspaper headline spelled out a threatening message:

> Larsens,
> Leave the Games now! If you don't go back to Norway, you're dead.

"Sigrid Larsen found this threat at the pool yesterday," Hewitt explained. "Someone had stuffed it under her towel."

"Who's Sigrid Larsen?" Nancy asked.

"The swimming star of the Norwegian team. Her twin brother, Ragnar, is an up-and-comer in the decathlon."

Frank put the paper down on Hewitt's desk. "I guess someone doesn't want them competing," he said.

"Any ideas who?" Nancy looked at Hewitt.

"A jealous competitor?" Joe suggested.

"Or someone in the Larsens' past who's out to get them," Bess added with a dramatic shudder.

"It could be anybody," Hewitt said, summing up the situation. "That's why I need help in finding him or her."

"Assuming that the person means the Larsens harm," Dr. Matthews said quietly. "He might simply be some prankster looking for publicity."

"We can't take that chance, Doc." Hewitt turned to Nancy. "I realize there isn't much to go on, but you've got to find him or her—and fast." Hewitt's despair was apparent as he turned away to look out his window.

"We'll do our best. Right, guys?" Nancy asked her friends. "It seems this is the best way for us to go—undercover."

Just then a young man knocked and strode into the room, a red-and-blue snugly fitting jacket across his broad shoulders. From his team colors and the flag patch on his left sleeve, Frank knew he must be a competitor from Norway.

"I don't care what my sister says, Mr. Hewitt," the blond-haired guy said, with a soft lilt in his voice. "We're not leaving. I'm not running back to Oslo because of some stupid threat!"

"Ragnar," Hewitt answered, getting up from his desk. "You'll be pleased to hear that we've taken steps to protect you and your sister. I'd like you to meet these people."

Hewitt introduced Ragnar to the Hardys, Nancy, Bess, and George. Ragnar's chiseled features seemed to soften when he met George.

"George—" he said, his hand lingering on hers. "Isn't that an odd name for a girl in English?"

George couldn't stop looking into Ragnar's glacial blue eyes. Her smile was shy. "Actually, my real name is Georgia."

"On you, they both sound pretty," Ragnar said with a grin.

For the first time in ages, Nancy saw a rosy blush spread across George's face.

While George and Ragnar talked, Nancy turned back to the others. "Maybe we should begin by talking to Sigrid. She may have noticed someone hanging out near her towel before she found that note."

"Good idea," Hewitt said, and raised his voice to get Ragnar's attention. "Is your sister finished with her practice session yet?" he asked him.

"She should be just returning to her room to

get ready for lunch," Ragnar said. "If you come with me, I'll show you where she's staying."

Hewitt told them to come back later for their undercover assignments. After he explained to Ragnar who Nancy, Bess, George, and the Hardys were, he cautioned him not to tell anyone why they were there.

"Is this your first trip to the States?" Nancy asked Ragnar on their way across the campus to Banning Hall.

"Yes." Ragnar smiled. "Sigrid and I have done most of our competing in Europe."

"Did your family come with you?" George asked.

"My grandfather raised us after our parents —passed away." Ragnar's face turned somber. "But he was away at sea a lot. Sometimes it was as if Sigrid and I had no family at all. Now he's dead and it is only us two."

"You must be very close," Nancy said.

Ragnar suddenly stopped and faced Nancy, his body rigid.

"Don't think I'm afraid of whoever left that note. Because I'm not. I only asked for protection because of Sigrid." His voice became quieter at the thought of his sister. "I can't let anything happen to her, I just can't."

Nancy reached out and touched his wrist. "We're all on the same side, Ragnar."

"Nancy only wants to help," George said.

Ragnar let out a deep sigh. "I know," he said. "I'm sorry. I've been under a lot of pressure lately. I trained all the time for the decathlon—too much maybe. And all competitions are important to me. I can't let a ridiculous threat chase me home."

"Of course not," George said as they entered Banning Hall and started up the stairs to Sigrid's room on the second floor.

Halfway up they heard a scream explode from a room down the hall.

They all reacted at once, racing up the few remaining stairs and down the hall to an open door.

Charging into the room first, Nancy saw a lovely blond girl standing beside the bed, trembling as she stared at the pillow in wide-eyed horror.

Nancy's gaze darted to the pillow.

There lay a color photo, a publicity shot of Ragnar Larsen. Someone had stuck a razor-sharp knife right through the middle of Ragnar's smiling face!

Chapter Three

SIGRID!" RAGNAR SHOUTED, and ran to his sister.

Sobbing, the girl turned and fell into her brother's arms. "Let's go home, Ragnar, please! He means to kill us!"

"Don't be silly," Ragnar said. "No one's going to kill us." He looked down and saw the mutilated photo. "It's only that stupid prankster." A muscle twitched just above his jaw.

"I want to go home." Sigrid clutched him tightly. "Everything is going wrong. First my coach got sick. Now someone's trying to kill us!"

Ragnar made a shushing noise. "No one's

urt us. It's just someone who wants of the Games. We can't let him scare us . Be brave. You're a Larsen, remember?"

Sigrid looked at her brother, her eyes full of tears. "I can't lose you, Ragnar," she said. "You're the only family I have left."

While Ragnar continued to comfort his sister, Nancy took out a handkerchief, covered her right hand, and picked up the knife.

"What do you think?" Frank asked, looking at the knife.

Nancy studied it carefully. "Looks like an ordinary penknife to me."

"And it doesn't tell us a thing," Frank said with a frown. He took the knife out of Nancy's hand and looked at it carefully.

Nancy saw Joe running his hands along the wrinkled bedspread. She was about to ask him what he was doing when Ragnar spoke up.

"I'd like to be alone with my sister for a while, if you don't mind."

"We understand." Nancy joined Bess and George, and they all slipped out into the hall.

"We'll be back later this afternoon," Frank promised, then followed Joe out.

"This is just awful," George said to Bess. "Who could be doing this to them?"

"I don't know, but I hope we find out who it is before anything really terrible happens," Bess answered.

As they headed down the corridor, Nancy

nudged Joe. "What did you find in there?" she asked.

"Not much gets past you, does it, Drew?" With a rueful grin, Joe reached into his shirt pocket and pulled out a piece of paper. "I found this near the pillow. I think our culprit put it on the photo, but it must have fallen off."

Nancy looked at it. It was a picture of a black horse-headed chess piece, carefully torn from a magazine.

"A black knight," Nancy murmured, showing the picture to Frank.

"I wonder what it means?" Frank asked, handing the photo back to Nancy. "I think we'd better show it to Glen Hewitt."

"And find out exactly what our assignments are," George put in.

"I hope it isn't anything too dangerous," Bess said as they all headed back to the security chief's office.

They found Hewitt seated at his desk, looking over some paperwork. "Back so soon?" he asked with a smile.

Nancy showed him the picture. "Is either Ragnar or Sigrid Larsen a chess player, by any chance?" Joe asked after Hewitt had looked at it.

Hewitt shrugged. "I don't know." Scowling at the picture, he added angrily, "Just what we need—an out-and-out lunatic!"

Nancy reminded herself to quiz Sigrid about the picture later.

"Well, let's get on to the assignments," Hewitt said, forgetting about the photograph and looking down at a list on his desk. "Frank, I want you working with me in Games security. Joe, I'm putting you on the Norwegians' track and field team. Sort of a glorified go-fer."

"Go-fer?" Bess asked.

"Yeah, you know, you 'go fer' this and 'go fer' that," Joe explained.

"This is great—Frank's in a suit and gets respect. I'm in sweatpants lugging around barbells," Joe groused.

Frank grinned at him. "A perfect division of labor."

"Nancy," Hewitt went on, "I'd like to put you and George on Sigrid's team. Could you pass as practice competitors?"

"Me against a top swimmer? All right!" George grinned eagerly.

"It'll work for George," Nancy said. "But I couldn't possibly compete with these girls." Nancy thought for a moment. "I know! I'll pretend to be a nutritionist, working with the Norwegians."

"Hey, aren't you forgetting somebody?" Bess complained.

They all turned to look at her. Glen Hewitt scanned his list. "I think I could put you with the American track team as a water girl," he said.

Bess's face fell. "I didn't want danger, but a water girl?"

Gripping Bess's shoulders, Nancy murmured in her ear. "Think of it, Bess—you'll spend all day talking to those gorgeous guys on the American team. Can't you just see yourself out there, pouring a nice cold glass of water for Dave Gillespie?"

Bess's mood changed from indignation to eager delight. "Well, when you put it that way . . ." She tugged impatiently at her friend's arm. "Let's hurry up and have lunch. I've got to get to work!"

After lunch an excited Bess rushed out to pick up her gear. Nancy and George returned to Sigrid's dorm room.

Nancy knocked softly. "Come in," Sigrid said.

Sigrid greeted them with a shy smile. Thick, corn-colored hair brushed her shoulders, and her eyes were the same clear blue as Ragnar's, but her classic high cheekbones, tapered chin, and soft, expressive mouth were unmistakably feminine. A royal blue bathing suit highlighted her slim, athletic figure.

"I want to apologize for my outburst before," Sigrid said. "Ragnar told me what you're doing for us. I'm very grateful. He also explained that I shouldn't tell anyone why you're here."

"You don't need to apologize," Nancy said, shaking Sigrid's extended hand. "But I do appreciate your protecting our identity. It's important that whoever is doing this doesn't think he's being watched."

Sigrid nodded. "I must get to the pool. I have a qualifying heat very soon."

George ran back to her room to put on a bathing suit and the three of them headed for the outdoor pool.

On their way over, Nancy asked Sigrid if either she or Ragnar played chess. She was thinking of that photo Joe had found.

Sigrid laughed. "Chess? No. We're both too impatient to play chess. Why do you ask?"

"No reason," Nancy said, frowning. If neither of them was a chess player, what was the meaning of that bizarre clue?

Before they entered the poolside area, Nancy could hear the din of shrill whistles and coaches shouting to the athletes. Nancy, George, and Sigrid had to walk the length of the Olympic-size swimming pool. Nancy could observe the other swimmers.

One blond girl appeared to be arguing in whispers with her middle-aged coach. Another was getting encouragement from her teammates. But the swimmer who caught Nancy's attention was a thin but muscular girl who kept tossing her long black hair and posing. She hardly looked like a serious competitor.

The girl who had been arguing with her coach recognized Sigrid and came over to greet her.

"I thought I knew all the girls on the team," she said to Sigrid, but watched Nancy and George with her sparkling sapphire eyes. She flipped her sun-streaked blond hair off her shoulders. "My name's Tracy Reynolds, by the way."

"I'm Sigrid's practice competitor, George Fayne. And I'm an American, too."

Nancy moved in right on cue. "Hi, I'm Nancy Drew." She added just the right note of professionalism to her voice. "I'm with the Havemeyer Institute."

Smiling uncertainly, Tracy shook Nancy's hand as another swimmer came over.

"Sigrid," the girl said. "What's this? A practice competitor?" The girl was rubbing a towel over her short platinum hair. A slow smile turned up her mouth but didn't reach her green eyes.

"George is going to help in the hundred-meter freestyle," Sigrid answered. "Nancy, George—Grete Nordstrom, Sweden."

"Won't Ragnar help you practice?" Grete's phony smile widened. "Don't tell me your brother's scared of the water."

Sigrid folded her towel and faced Grete. "My brother's not a swimmer. George is. Now, don't you think you should get ready?"

As Grete walked away, Nancy turned to Sigrid. "What was that all about?"

"Oh, she's angry because she used to date Ragnar and it didn't work out. But she can't seem to forget it."

The girls warmed up, and a few minutes later a whistle blew. Nancy saw the striped shirt of a referee at the far corner of the pool.

"This afternoon's event is a preliminary qualifying heat," the referee announced, clipboard in hand. "We will begin in five minutes."

Sigrid pointed to show Nancy and George how to get to the grandstand. Then she headed for the starting blocks.

At the far end of the pool, Nancy heard a female voice in her ear. "Having fun?" it said.

Turning, Nancy found herself looking at a stunning raven-haired swimmer. The girl had a lovely face with an aquiline nose, a broad, full mouth, and eyes like wet black jewels. A bright blue racing suit called attention to her flawless figure. Grinning at Nancy, she swung her tanned arms around in circles, loosening up her shoulders.

"You're Rosalia, aren't you?" George asked. She'd read about the flamboyant swimmer in the sports pages.

"Uh-huh. Rosalia Vargas. Remember that name. You'll be seeing my face on a movie screen someday." Eyes narrowing, Rosalia looked at the other end of the pool. "Look at that! Princess Grete's giving orders to her ladies-in-waiting."

"Shouldn't you be over there, too?" Nancy asked.

"Soon. I have to make my entrance," she said without apology.

A murmur rose from the spectators, and Nancy saw the referee glancing impatiently at his watch. Smiling in satisfaction, Rosalia sauntered slowly toward the starting blocks.

"Oh, I'm so sorry," Nancy heard her say as she went to step up to her starting block. Finally, she was in place.

The referee's whistle trilled. The ten competitors came forward, forming a ragged line as the Games supervisor called out their names.

Nancy found an empty seat in the stands just as the second whistle sounded. Turning, she saw Sigrid with the others, leaning over into her assigned lane. Ten splashes simultaneously broke the pool's placid surface.

The competition was on.

Later that afternoon Nancy followed George, Sigrid, and Grete to the women's locker room next to the pool. In their short walk Nancy heard the noise of buzz saws and hammers from inside the nearby stadium. Looking over, Nancy saw hard-hatted workmen wrestling great lengths of boards into the stadium.

"What are they doing?" Nancy asked.

Grete looked up. "I'm not sure."

"It looks to me like they might be replacing some bleachers," George said. "Remember that section that was off-bounds—it had yellow tape blocking it off. And the Games begin in three days."

Stopping at the locker room door, Grete turned to Nancy and George. "Are you going to the welcoming banquet?" The girls nodded. "Why don't you join my boyfriend and me?"

Nancy felt a tingle of anticipation. She hadn't even gotten a chance to see *her* boyfriend yet. "We can walk over with you, but Dave Gillespie is our host. Do you think it'd be okay if I brought a date?"

"I guess so. Check with Mr. Overton to be sure. We'll all meet at my boyfriend's room at six sharp. Lino Passano, room four-fourteen, Rondileau Hall."

Grete left them to head for the showers, and Sigrid turned to George as they strolled into the tiled locker room. "You know, you ought to get into league competition."

George grimaced. "No way! I'm much too

slow. I swallowed your wake all the way to the finish line."

"All you need is practice, George," Sigrid said, walking up to her locker.

"I'll try to remember that." George let out a weary groan. "Right now, I need a shower."

Sigrid yanked her door open. "I'll be with you in a minute. First I want to—"

The girl's voice suddenly faded. Nancy turned to see Sigrid standing transfixed in front of her open locker. A look of horror distorted her pretty face.

Then, her eyes rolling upward, Sigrid toppled to the floor in a dead faint!

Chapter Four

NANCY FELL TO HER KNEES beside Sigrid and saw with relief that the girl's eyelids were fluttering.

"What happened?" George asked.

"She fainted." Nancy grabbed a towel from Sigrid's locker and made a pillow for the girl's head. "There's a first-aid box outside the locker room, George. See if you can find some smelling salts."

"Right!" George hurried off.

After she made sure that Sigrid was as comfortable as possible and was breathing normally, Nancy stood up to check the girl's locker. There she saw the reason for Sigrid's sudden fainting spell.

A small black chess piece, a knight, dangled from the lace of a sneaker. Nancy thought immediately of the photograph cut out from a magazine that Joe had found on Sigrid's bed.

What did it mean? Nancy wondered. Sigrid was terrified, but why? What could be so frightening about a small black knight?

George came back, holding a bottle. "I found some," she said.

Nancy unscrewed the plastic cap and held the smelling salts under Sigrid's nose. The girl tossed her head restlessly, and Sigrid let out a small whimper.

"Relax," Nancy said. "You're going to be all right."

Sigrid's eyes fluttered open and she murmured a strange word. It sounded to Nancy like *ridder.*

Nancy and George helped Sigrid sit up on a bench. George gently asked, "What made you pass out?"

A terrified look crossed Sigrid's face as she remembered what had happened. Her glance fell on the open locker.

"I think I know." Covering her hand with a towel, Nancy yanked the chess piece free and showed it to George. "The phantom prankster strikes again."

Nancy took a long look at the chess piece. Because there was no seam down the spine, she assumed it must have been hand-carved. She wrapped it in the towel. Evidence for fingerprinting, she thought. Then she turned to Sigrid.

"You said something when you were coming to," she said. "It sounded like *ridder*. What did you mean?"

Sigrid hesitated, wide-eyed. Then, with a slight shudder, she said, "I don't know," and stood up. "Thank you for helping me," she said. "I think I'll take a shower now." She picked up a towel and headed for the shower.

Nancy and George exchanged a look. "What's up, Nan?" George asked.

"I'm not sure." Nancy furrowed her brow. "But I don't think Sigrid was completely honest with us just now. She knows what *ridder* means, but she doesn't want to tell us."

"Why not?"

"Your guess is as good as mine," Nancy said, closing the door to Sigrid's locker.

Ridder . . .

Nancy wondered what it could be? A place? A thing? Someone's name? And why wouldn't Sigrid talk about it?

Joe Hardy leaned over to pick up a cantaloupe-size steel shot, letting his glance circle the practice field. Ragnar lay on the grass twenty feet away, grinding out sit-ups. His trainer shouted at him to pick up the pace.

Across the field, Joe could see Bess Marvin talking animatedly with Dave Gillespie. As Bess poured him a cold drink, Dave playfully mussed her hair.

I'm glad somebody's enjoying their work, Joe thought as he dropped the shot into his canvas tote bag.

Joe found his gaze drawn to an intense young man with shoulder-length blond hair whose face was ruddy behind steel-rimmed glasses. The boy was pumping out push-ups like a well-oiled machine.

"Impressive, don't you think?" Jim Overton had appeared at Joe's side.

"You bet," Joe said. "He's up to thirty a minute by my count. Who is he anyway?"

"Kurt Schweigert. He's only nineteen but in Germany he's known as the Man of Steel."

Joe let out a low whistle. "I've read about him. Hasn't he broken all the records in the men's fifteen hundred meters?"

"You bet," Overton said, nodding. "But he's worried because his standing took a tumble when he pulled a thigh muscle in his last big competition." Overton looked over to where Dave Gillespie was still talking to Bess. "He's got to win this one, but it won't be easy. Because of Dave and Ragnar, Kurt has some tough competition this year."

Joe and Overton had started walking toward the benches when two more decathlon athletes came running over to them. One was a muscular, olive-skinned boy with deep-set black eyes that matched his unruly black hair. The other looked like his opposite: he was tall and had blond hair and watery blue eyes.

"Ciao, Mr. Overton," the dark-haired boy said, giving Overton a dazzling smile.

"Joe Hardy, Lino Passano from Italy. And this is Britain's Jeffrey Cannon."

Jeff's smile and handshake were a little formal. "Hello."

"Giuseppe, nice to meet you," Lino said, enthusiastically pumping Joe's hand.

"Don't forget your appointment with Dr. Matthews, Lino," Overton said.

Lino groaned. Overton's voice was deadly serious. "You know the rules," he said.

Joe frowned to himself, wondering what Lino had against being tested. He must be used to it by now, he thought. It was standard practice in sports competitions.

"Couldn't be that Lino's afraid of a little needle, could it?" Jeffrey Cannon asked.

Lino laughed. "Who isn't? Ever since I was a kid, I've hated them. But I'll be there. I won't like it, but I'll be there."

"Good." Overton turned to Joe. "Let's introduce you around," he said.

"Sounds good to me." Joe said goodbye to Lino and Jeff and followed Overton to the nearby benches where he had seen Bess and Dave.

"Hi, Joe." Bess smiled and opened a soda can. "Here, you look like you could use this."

Thanks for blowing my cover, Bess, Joe thought.

"You know each other?" Dave asked. He lifted his head as his coach massaged his neck muscles.

Bess beamed. "Oh, we've known each other since—"

"Since we worked at a resort together on Padre Island," Joe interrupted. He shot Bess a warning look. "Right?"

"R-right," Bess stammered, trying to cover herself. Luckily, she realized she should change the subject. "Joe, you wouldn't believe how Dave and I met. He was practicing his javelin throw."

Dave stood up and seemed to force a smile on his face. "Hey, Bess, it wasn't any big deal. I'm sure Joe here doesn't want to hear all the gory details."

"Sure he does." Bess went on. "I was standing right over there, next to the bleachers. After Dave threw the javelin the wind must have taken it—"

Joe watched Dave's reaction. The boy anxiously wet his lips. He also looked as if he wanted to clamp both his hands over Bess's mouth.

"Because before I knew it, the javelin was heading straight for me. If it hadn't been for Nancy, I don't know what would have happened."

"You ought to be more careful," Joe told Bess, still keeping an eye on Dave.

"It was an accident," Dave said softly, nervously rubbing the back of his neck.

Overton spoke up. "You do that in the Games, Dave, and you're through. I'll have to show you a few wrist exercises. You could use more control."

"Sounds good," Dave said, getting up from the bench. "See you then. Let's go, Bess. I need a cold drink."

"But, Dave," Bess said, pointing under the bench. "You have all the water you need right here."

Dave gently put his hand on her elbow. "I know," Joe heard him say. "But I want one with you alone."

Bess smiled sheepishly, then waved goodbye to Joe. "See you later," she said.

Joe watched them walk away and made up his mind to ask Nancy about what Bess had just told him. It might be nothing, but it seemed to him that something was not quite right.

"I've got to get back to work," Overton said, interrupting Joe's thoughts. "But I'll see you at the banquet tonight, right?"

"Banquet? Oh, right." He remembered Hewitt having said something about a welcoming banquet that night. "I'll be there," he told Overton.

Joe was heading back to the Norwegians when he saw his brother standing beside Ragnar and his coach. When he reached them, he overheard Ragnar talking to Olaf, his coach.

"Be reasonable," Ragnar was saying. "I'm tired."

Pointing at the bleachers, his coach snapped, "Do it!"

Ragnar scowled. "I told you, there's nothing wrong with my legs."

"You need to work on your endurance," Olaf said gruffly. "Otherwise, Schweigert and Gillespie are going to clobber you in the fifteen hundred meters."

Joe saw the muscles in Ragnar's jaw tighten before he ran across the field and up the bleacher steps, three at a time.

"What's up?" Joe asked after moving aside with his brother and Hewitt, who had just joined them.

After blowing his nose, Hewitt answered. "I had a call from Nancy," he said. "Seems that someone left Sigrid a present in her locker."

"What kind of present?" Joe asked.

"A chess piece—a black knight, to be more specific. It looks like our lunatic has struck again."

Frank and Joe exchanged a look. "Did you send out that knife we found for fingerprints?" Frank asked.

Hewitt nodded. "Yes, but it was clean. Whoever is behind this knows what he's doing."

"Anything happen with Ragnar, Joe?" Frank asked.

"Not a thing. It's been real quiet. It looks like Sigrid is the target." Then he remembered what Bess had told him. "But Bess mentioned something about Dave Gillespie accidentally throwing a javelin at her."

Frank looked confused, but Glen Hewitt's eyes widened.

"Is something wrong?" Joe asked Hewitt. "Dave did say it was an accident."

Hewitt lowered his voice so no one around them could hear. "I think I should tell you—two years ago, Dave Gillespie may have killed a man."

Chapter Five

"WHAT?" Joe thought back to Dave's reaction when Bess was telling her story. So that's why he'd looked so nervous!

"He may have been responsible for the death of one of his classmates," Hewitt said grimly. "A boy named Juan Valverde."

"That's pretty heavy," Frank said. "Where did you hear it?"

Hewitt looked around and blew his nose once before continuing. "I investigated the case myself, boys, so it's not just an accusation. It was two years ago, while I was still chief of detectives in Santa Teresa."

"Maybe we'd better sit down," Frank said. He led Joe and Hewitt over to some empty bleachers.

"So what's the story?" Joe asked when they were sitting.

"Dave Gillespie's a local boy," Hewitt explained. "Born and raised here. He was the hottest thing that ever hit Santa Teresa High School. Football, baseball, track—you name it. He turned down sports scholarships to some big schools to concentrate on the decathlon."

Frank raised his eyebrows. "Really? I'm surprised. A scholarship like that is practically a ticket to the pros."

"Dave said he was never interested in pro football or baseball. He's only wanted to be an Olympic decathlon superstar. Anyway, Dave had one big rival at Santa Teresa: Juan Valverde."

"How bad was the rivalry?" Joe asked.

"Pretty bad. They competed for all the same things, even girls. They once had a fistfight in a parking lot after a dance." He shook his head at the memory.

"What happened?" Frank prodded.

"Things came to a head. Dave challenged Juan to a cross-country race—just the two of them. In the middle, about halfway up Mount Sabado, Juan passed out. Dave ran to the nearest house to call for help, but it was too late. Juan died during the helicopter ride to the hospital."

"It may be rare, but that can happen to athletes," Frank said. "What makes you think it was foul play?"

"I didn't at first." Hewitt pursed his lips, then bit the lower one. "Until Juan's younger sister came in and told me she thought Juan had been murdered. I did a routine investigation and came up with some interesting facts."

"Such as?" Joe asked. He was squinting into the fading sunlight, watching the athletes finish up for the day.

"Juan had a slight congenital heart defect, which Dave could have known about because he worked at the hospital where Juan's medical records were kept."

"So?" Frank and Joe were beginning to think that Hewitt was grasping at straws.

Hewitt sensed their disbelief. "I know it sounds crazy, but then there was the canteen."

"What canteen?" Joe asked.

"Juan was seen drinking from a canteen just before the race, but I walked every inch of the stretch he and Dave ran, and I never found it. It just disappeared."

Frank gave Hewitt a long, speculative look. "You think somebody poisoned the canteen?"

"It's possible, Frank."

"And Dave Gillespie was your prime suspect?" Joe asked.

"He was on the scene and he was Juan's biggest rival," Hewitt replied. "He could have slipped something into that canteen when Juan wasn't looking."

"It's one conclusion," Frank said, rubbing his chin thoughtfully. "But without that canteen, you don't have a case."

Hewitt sighed, then shook his head. "I know. That's what the DA told me. No direct chain of evidence. A sister's accusation and a missing canteen don't add up to murder."

"You really think Gillespie could have murdered him?" Frank asked. He still needed to be convinced.

"I don't know what to think," Hewitt said, standing up. "But I can tell you two things: Dave Gillespie acted really suspicious when I questioned him, and he's been evasive ever since."

"You still haven't forgotten it, have you?" Joe asked.

"No. I pride myself on my ability to read people. I was a cop for a long time. There was more to that race up Sabado than a simple grudge match, I can feel it in my gut." Hewitt patted his belly. "Someday I'm going to find out what really happened."

"Well, thanks for telling us about it," Frank said. "You never know, it may be relevant."

"You never know," Hewitt repeated. "See

you boys later." He stepped off the bleachers and headed back toward his office.

"What do you think?" Joe asked as he and Frank strolled out of the stadium toward their dorm. Around them, weary athletes were also heading home for the day.

"It all sounds pretty farfetched," Frank said. "But we can't dismiss it entirely."

Joe nodded. "You're right. It's possible to cause a heart attack with drugs. Maybe Gillespie knew how to do it, or he had someone do it for him. Still, it seems like a really drastic thing to do."

"I agree," Frank nodded. He flashed his brother a quizzical look. "Are you thinking what I'm thinking?" he asked.

"You must have read my mind," Joe groaned. "Yet another mystery at Santa Teresa."

Frank's mouth curved into a grim smile. "Welcome to the Juan Valverde case."

Nancy stood before her dresser mirror, carefully fastening a gold hoop earring. She'd changed out of her casual clothes into a soft slate blue silk dress. As she was taking one last look, the phone rang.

"I'll get it, George."

"Hi, beautiful. And a belated welcome to Southern California." Ned's voice was warm and tender.

"Ned! Finally. We kept missing each other. I was wondering when we'd finally connect." Nancy smiled.

"Sorry," Ned said. "I wanted to meet you this morning, but I got called back to the office. We're running checks on all the athletes' beneficiaries." He groaned slightly. "Do you have any idea how many kids are competing in the Games?"

Nancy laughed. "Well, you can rest up tonight at the banquet. You got my message about it, didn't you?"

"I did, and I wouldn't miss it for anything. I just hope I don't fall asleep on you."

"I'll do my best to keep you awake, Ned Nickerson. By the way, we're double dating."

"With whom?"

"Grete Nordstrom and Lino Passano. We're meeting at Lino's room at six o'clock. He's in Rondileau Hall, room four-fourteen."

"Okay. See you there. Hey, by the way, what's up with the Larsens?"

"I'll fill you in tonight," Nancy said. "Take care, Nickerson."

"Love you, Drew. So long."

Nancy was hanging up the phone as George came out of the bathroom, straightening the shoulders of her beaded turquoise top. Bess had left earlier with Dave Gillespie.

"That had to be Ned," George said with a smile as she reached for her purse. "He's the only one who makes your eyes shine like that."

Nancy blushed and tried not to laugh. "You're getting to be a real detective, George Fayne. Come on, I told Sigrid we'd stop by for her before we meet Lino and Grete."

They left their room, and within a few seconds, Nancy was knocking on Sigrid's door.

"Who's there?" a timid voice called out.

"It's Nancy and George," Nancy said.

A deadbolt was slid open, and the door swung wide. Sigrid faced them in a white bathrobe, her face and body tense. "It's you. Please come in."

Nancy and George stepped inside, and Sigrid closed the door and clicked the bolt into place. Her dress was lying on the bed.

"You better hurry and get ready," George urged.

Sigrid looked a little embarrassed. "I'm sorry. I lost track of the time. I was thinking—"

"About what, Sigrid? *Ridder?*" Nancy tried to keep her tone soft, but she had to find out what was going on.

The suggestion took Sigrid by surprise. She gasped, and a look of terror clouded over her blue eyes.

"We want to help you," Nancy went on. She touched the girl's arm sympathetically. "You've got to trust us. Why did you say the word *ridder?* What does it mean?"

With tears in her eyes, Sigrid sat down on the bed. "He's going to kill Ragnar," she said in a frightened little voice. "And nothing will stop him. He's a demon!"

Nancy looked at George in confusion. "Maybe you should explain what this is all about," she said.

"It has to do with an old Norse tale," Sigrid said. "Hundreds of years ago the king of Norway died and left his infant son on the throne. Then a traitor took power and tried to kill the baby."

Nancy could tell that now was not the time to ask Sigrid what a fairy tale had to do with the threats. She let her go on.

"Two woodsmen put the baby in a sack and carried him to safety in the mountains. The traitor looked everywhere for him—unsuccessfully. Then he came to our town, Narvik, to ask Gudrun, a powerful sorceress, for help. He wanted her to use her magic to kill the child. She agreed, saying, 'You shall have a knight to do this deed.' "

"Then what happened?" Nancy asked.

"That night there was a terrible storm, and several people said they saw Gudrun in the cemetery. She came back at dawn with a man by her side, a tall man in black knight's armor, wearing a long black cloak. *Ridder!*"

With a fearful whisper, Sigrid went on. "When some townspeople went out to the cemetery they found an old grave dug open and the body missing. Gudrun had brought the dead man to life, and he became her servant, Ridder, which means 'knight' in Norwegian." Sigrid's haunted eyes met Nancy's. "Gudrun commanded Ridder to find the baby. He roamed the entire country and searched everywhere, but there was no trace of the child."

Sigrid took a deep breath and continued. "The traitor was very angry. He told Gudrun, 'You have not kept your promise.' But Gudrun's powers were great, and she had never failed before. She told the traitor, 'My black knight will search until he performs the deed you ask. And where Ridder has been, he will leave a single chess piece—' "

"A black knight?" Nancy asked quietly.

Sigrid nodded slowly. "They say Ridder still wanders in the mountains, searching for the king's infant son, and as long as a prince of Norway lives, he'll never return to his grave."

"But that's just a story," George said after a moment.

Nancy gave George a look. Obviously there was something about this fairy tale that had Sigrid in its grip.

"I'm not sure I understand," Nancy said to Sigrid. "What does this have to do with you and Ragnar?"

Sigrid went to her nightstand. She handed

Nancy and George a Norwegian newspaper, pointing out the headline.

"This says, 'Ragnar Larsen—Prince of Norwegian Sport'!" She translated the headline. Then tears filled her eyes. "That's what everyone calls him back home: the Prince of Sports. And because he's a 'prince,' Ridder has come to America to kill him!" Sigrid began to sob.

None of this makes any sense, Nancy thought as she reached out to comfort Sigrid. A ghostly assassin from the Middle Ages? Why would this killer come after Ragnar simply because he was known as the Prince of Sports? Although it didn't seem possible that anyone could believe the story, Sigrid clearly did.

George whispered to Nancy. "Why don't you go on ahead? Grete's probably waiting for us. I'll take care of Sigrid."

"All right, George," Nancy said. "Grete probably is worried. Will you be okay, Sigrid?" she asked.

Sigrid nodded. "I'm so glad I finally told someone. Now maybe we can do something to stop Ridder."

"I'm sure we can," Nancy said as she left the room and headed down the stairs and outside. Five minutes later she was rushing through the empty lobby of Rondileau Hall. A glance at the lobby clock told her it was already six-ten.

She took the elevator up to the fourth floor,

and her footsteps echoed off the walls as she approached Lino's room.

The door was open. Peering inside, Nancy saw there was no one in the room. Ned must have gotten tied up, but where were Grete and Lino?

Nancy's attention then was drawn by an open chess board that lay on the desk. In neat rows, opposing chessmen faced one another. Nancy stepped inside, compelled by something her eyes had caught. The board was incomplete.

A chill passed over her. Both of the set's black knights were missing!

Chapter Six

NANCY WALKED all the way to the desk. "Anyone home?" she asked.

There was no answer. Nancy let her gaze circle the room, noticing the clothes strewn carelessly around, the expensive portable stereo system, and a colorful poster on the wall.

With a tissue, Nancy pulled the black knight she'd found in Sigrid's locker from her purse. She carefully picked up a white knight.

Holding the two up, she could tell they were a perfect match. The black knight appeared to have come from this very set.

The sound of male voices in the hall turned Nancy around. Standing in the doorway were two boys, wearing nothing but towels wrapped around their waists.

"I say!" Jeff Cannon's blush matched the crimson on Nancy's face.

Lino was nearly speechless. "Excuse me, but who are you?" he finally asked.

Nancy kept her eyes firmly on his face. "My name's Nancy Drew," she managed to say. "I was supposed to meet Grete here." For some reason, Nancy couldn't remember Grete's last name.

Jeff took off with a "pleased to meet you." Pulling his towel tight around his waist, Lino looked at Nancy.

"Lino Passano," he said, adding, "so where's Grete? Why did she tell you to meet me here?"

"I'm not sure," Nancy said, offering him a glassy smile. "But, well, the door was open, and I, um, saw your chess set and wanted to take a closer look."

To Nancy the excuse sounded a little lame, but Lino's smile broadened. "You're a chess fanatic, I suppose?"

Realizing that she was going to be trapped in her lie, Nancy decided to be honest. "Actually," she said, "I was curious about the two missing pieces—the black knights."

Lino glanced at the board, his eyes flickering in surprise. "What are you talking about? There are no missing pieces. Oh," he said, noticing the board, "there is one piece missing. But only one."

"That's because I put this one back a moment ago." Nancy went to the set and picked up the black knight she had taken from Sigrid's locker. "I found it hanging in Sigrid Larsen's locker. And I'm wondering how it got there." She looked for Lino's reaction.

He burst into laughter and tried to snatch the chess piece away. But Nancy was too quick for him.

"You think I did it?" he asked incredulously.

"Well, it is yours," she said.

"And you think I went running through the girls' locker room in my towel? I've been in the shower for the last twenty minutes. Before that I was running a fifteen-hundred-meter with Jeff."

Nancy considered Lino's alibi. He hadn't given her an alibi for the right time. He had to be innocent—or was he just clever. Then something else occurred to Nancy. "Do you always keep your door unlocked?" she asked, ready to leave.

"When I'm in the boys' dorm, taking a shower down the hall—sure!" With a slight smile, he slowly closed the door on Nancy. "From now on, though, I suppose I should lock it. Now, if you don't mind, I'd like to get dressed."

"Be my guest," Nancy said. She tucked the

black knight into her purse before Lino could ask for it back and hurried down the corridor. If he left his door unlocked often, anyone could have stolen the chess pieces.

Nancy pushed the elevator's Down button. When the elevator doors slid open, Ned Nickerson was standing there, beaming at her.

"You look great," he said, holding out his arms. "No, you look better than great—you look perfect." Nancy slid into Ned's arms and pulled her head back to receive Ned's kiss. The two of them clung together for a long moment. Finally, with a mutual sigh, they parted.

Nancy brushed Ned's cheek with her fingertips. "It's been a long two weeks."

"You said it. Hey," Ned said, looking around. "Where're the people we're supposed to meet?"

Nancy put her arm through Ned's and pushed the button for the elevator again. "Lino's up here still. I think we'd better head off Grete downstairs. I just made a terrific first impression on her boyfriend." Nancy felt herself blushing again.

"What happened?"

"I'll fill you in on the way to the banquet. But don't you dare laugh when I tell you!"

Arm in arm Ned and Nancy strolled the perimeter of the sprawling dining room in the student union building, where the official welcoming Games banquet was being held. Waiters moved among cloth-covered tables, and small groups of athletes congregated at the tables and along the walls, quietly talking.

George was sitting with Ragnar and Sigrid. She was demure yet striking in a long peach-colored silk dress.

"Sigrid looks a little wiped out," Nancy whispered in Ned's ear as they leaned against a wall not far from their table. "But I guess I'd be wiped out, too, if I'd been through what she's been through today."

Nancy quickly told Ned about the wooden and paper chess pieces and how they'd been left for Sigrid to find. "But I'm glad George was able to convince her to come. Sigrid really needs the opportunity to unwind."

"Nancy, you don't really believe this 'Killer from Beyond' story, do you?"

Nancy shook her head. "I'm too old for Halloween, Ned. But Sigrid believes it, and the culprit knows she does."

Ned nuzzled the back of her ear. "Tell you what," he said, "let's punch the time clock on detecting for the evening, okay?"

"That's a great idea," Nancy said, nestling her head on his shoulder. "I really have missed you, Ned."

"Let's see what we can do about it," Ned said, smiling. He tilted his head just then. "Look over there."

Following Ned's glance, Nancy saw Rosalia Vargas standing in the middle of a circle of boys. Her skin-tight white miniskirt and off-the-shoulder black knit top were guaranteed to draw attention.

Ned grinned. "I see the future movie star is having a good time."

"Oh?" Nancy felt just a twinge of jealousy. "I didn't realize you knew her."

Ned continued to watch Rosalia. "We met in Mr. Hewitt's office yesterday." Ned shook his head ruefully. "Rosalia's best friend is her mirror, and the great love of her life is movies. Nancy, you're looking at the next star of stage and screen."

"She told you all that?" Nancy flashed Ned an incredulous look.

Ned turned back to Nancy. "All she ever does is talk about herself. I kept trying to yawn with my mouth shut," he said.

Remembering her own meeting with Rosalia, Nancy giggled. Then she saw Frank and Joe Hardy walk into the room, dressed in lightweight blazers and dress slacks. Grinning, Joe waved in their direction.

"Frank and Joe?" Ned glanced quizzically at Nancy. "What are they doing here?"

"Glen Hewitt asked them to come, too, Ned. He's an old friend of their father's."

Before Ned could reply, Bess appeared, dragging Dave Gillespie over to meet them.

After introducing Ned to Dave, Bess turned to Nancy.

"So you finally solved the case of the missing boyfriend?" she asked with a laugh.

Nancy smiled. "The easiest one ever."

"George is saving places for us." Bess grinned in anticipation. "And I'm putting my diet on hold for tonight. Let's eat!"

Bess led them to the circular table where George, the Larsens, and Tracy Reynolds were already sitting. After they had sat down, a waiter wheeled a steaming cart loaded with plates to their table. Nancy took her napkin from the table and looked up to see Jim Overton on his way to the speaker's podium.

A ripple of applause circled the room. Overton smiled, tapped the microphone, and began his speech.

"I know how boring after-dinner speakers can be, so I thought I'd get this over with before dinner. On behalf of our sponsor, Zip Sportswear, I'd like to welcome you all. We're looking forward to some record-breaking competition here in Santa Teresa. And for you athletes, we've prepared individually designed meals. But nothing too rich or too fattening. There's dancing in the lounge afterward, but don't—I repeat don't—sprain or pull anything on the dance floor." Overton paused while the audience broke into laughter. "I've bored you enough. Enjoy tonight. And may the best women and men win!"

Overton sat down to a round of enthusiastic applause. Dave cut loose with a shrill whistle. "Now, there's a guy who knows how to make a speech," he said.

Tracy giggled. "Not your old coach, right, Dave?"

"Don't remind me," Dave said, taking his plate from the waiter. "Krulak used to go on for hours."

Nancy reached for her steak knife. "Did you grow up here in Santa Teresa, Tracy?"

"Nope. I'm actually from Palm Springs. But my aunt Marcy has a condo over in Mission Beach, and my parents let me move in with her three years ago."

"Good thing she did, too." Dave picked up the parsley centerpiece from the top of his steak.

"Why's that?" Ned asked.

"Santa Teresa's swim team was at the bottom of the league before Tracy came to town. She made us state champs by the end of her senior year."

"Careful, Dave," Tracy said with a smile. "You'll have me blushing."

"Where do you train?" Sigrid asked.

"In the ocean. My coach put me onto it," Tracy answered.

Smiling, Sigrid took the last plate from the waiter. "Really? I thought I was the only one who did that."

"What ocean do you swim in?" Tracy asked.

"The North Sea." Sigrid's smile broadened. "I wait until the tide starts to run, then I swim across the mouth of Narvik Fjord. The pull of the outgoing tide strengthens my muscles."

Bess shivered. "The North Sea! How do you stand the cold?"

"Really," George added. "Don't you have icebergs up there?"

Nancy was happy to see Sigrid laughing out loud. She was being cheerful at last.

"Yes, we do," Sigrid answered. "Icebergs and seals and an occasional walrus even. But I wear a wetsuit so the cold doesn't—"

Nancy looked up to see what had cut the girl off. Sigrid was staring at her steak's centerpiece. Her features whitened in fright.

A tiny horse-headed object lay in the middle of Sigrid's plate.

The second black knight!

Chapter Seven

SIGRID LET OUT A SHRIEK and hysterically lunged to her feet, trying to get away.

Ragnar saw what had happened. He seized her firmly by the arm and murmured softly to her, trying to calm her down.

"Sigrid, please, it's nothing. Try to control yourself," he said.

Her eyes wide with fear, Sigrid snapped, "Ragnar, you know what this means!"

"Please excuse us," Ragnar said. He held Sigrid by the arm and guided her out the nearest door.

Nancy picked up the chess piece and whispered to Ned that she'd be back. Aware of the curious looks around her, she left the table, the Hardys close behind.

"We'll talk to the waiter and the kitchen staff," Frank whispered to her as they passed.

Nancy headed off in the direction the Larsens had taken. Walking out of the dining room and into a room with vending machines, she heard Sigrid's voice. She took care to stay out of sight, hoping to overhear their conversation.

"We should never have come here, Ragnar," Sigrid was saying. "Let's go home, please. We'll be safe there. Ridder will leave us alone."

"Sigrid, will you please get a grip on yourself? There's no such thing as Ridder. He's a myth! Can't you see what's going on?"

"He wants to kill us!" Sigrid cried.

"No, he doesn't. He's only trying to scare us off. Kurt knows he can't win if I'm competing, so he's using Ridder to force us to go home."

"Ragnar, Kurt Schweigert would never—"

"Open your eyes, Sigrid. It's so obvious. Schweigert never forgave me for beating him in Budapest last year. He's got to win this decathlon, or he's finished. It's Schweigert all right." There was an edge to Ragnar's voice.

"No, no, Ragnar. It's Ridder!"

"Stop being ridiculous! It's Kurt."

"How could he get past dozens of people and put that black knight on my steak? How could he slip unseen into the girls' locker room? It's got to be Ridder. A ghost can go anywhere."

"Sigrid, will you listen to yourself for a minute? You're sounding crazy."

"It's all true. Varmor says—"

"Varmor! Our old nurse. So that's where all this nonsense is coming from. That old woman told you too many fairy tales." Ragnar's voice had become calmer now. "Look, there's no reason for us to leave. No one has hurt us—"

"Yet!" Sigrid added forcefully.

"And no one will," Ragnar went on. "It's just a silly threat, that's all." Nancy heard Ragnar's weary sigh. "We can't leave, Sigrid. Norway is depending on us. We've got to stay and win. Now, come on, let's go back inside."

The sound of footsteps told Nancy that they were heading her way. She quickly ducked behind a nearby soda machine, then watched as Ragnar led Sigrid back into the dining room.

Nancy waited until they were out of sight, then she glanced at the chess piece again. She was almost positive it had come from Lino's set, but she'd have to compare it to the one she had in her purse to be sure.

Frank hailed Nancy as she was on her way back to the dining room. She waited for him at the door.

"What did you find out?" she asked him.

"The caterers brought the meals in right off

a truck. They loaded the carts in the kitchen. Each of the athletes' plates was tagged so special dietary considerations could be met."

Nancy frowned. "So there would be no trouble in finding her dinner plate."

Joe wandered up to them. "No one saw anything suspicious in the kitchen, and once the plates were out in the dining room, anybody could have walked past the tray and put the piece in Sigrid's steak."

"Not just anybody, Joe," Frank reminded him. "Only the athletes, caterers, and guests are allowed in here tonight. Chances are 'Ridder' is one of the athletes or guests. The three of us need to sit down and kick around some ideas. Tomorrow, though. Let's get back inside there before we blow our cover completely."

The next morning Nancy was sitting in the top row of stadium bleachers. She'd arranged to meet Frank and Joe there, and while she waited, she leaned her head back and basked in the hot California sun. A moist Pacific breeze ruffled her reddish blond hair.

"Nice weather, eh?" Frank Hardy said, jogging up the bleachers. "I see you managed to get away."

Nancy held her hand up to shield the sun from her eyes. "It wasn't hard. No one pays much attention to a nutritionist." She gave him a smile. "So how've you been?"

"Good. Joe and I have been busy since Padre Island." Frank loosened his tie, then undid his top shirt button. "Boy, is it ever hot!"

Below them, footsteps rattled the bleachers. Nancy heard Joe's voice. "You think it's hot up here, Frank? You ought to be down on the field. That Olaf is merciless. He runs me around almost as much as he does Ragnar."

"In that case, you'd better sit down and take a load off," he said, patting the seat next to him.

Joe plopped down with a soft groan.

"So what have we got?" Frank asked.

"A threatening note, a picture of a black knight, and two black knights," Nancy answered. She filled them in on Ridder and described her meeting with Lino Passano. "Both chess pieces appear to have come from Lino's set," she concluded.

"I was near him almost all day yesterday," Joe said. "I don't know when he could have done it—unless it was early, before we got on the case."

"And," Frank added, "anyone could have sneaked into his room."

Joe scowled. "But he was pretty upset about taking that steroids test. Maybe he does have something to hide."

"What's that got to do with Ridder, though?" Frank asked.

"Maybe Lino knows he can't beat Ragnar Larsen," Joe said, shrugging. "Maybe he's taking steroids to build up for the decathlon. If he scares Ragnar into dropping out, he's got a better shot."

"Lino's not the only one with that motive, Joe," Nancy pointed out. "Ragnar said the same thing about Kurt Schweigert."

"Interesting." Frank's eyes narrowed. "If we count Dave Gillespie, then that makes three suspects with the same motive. Also, Hewitt thinks Dave may have been responsible for the death of one of his high school classmates two years ago."

"What?"

Frank quickly outlined what Hewitt had told them about Juan Valverde.

"But what I don't understand is if the culprit wants Ragnar out of the games, why not go after Ragnar himself?" Nancy asked, thinking aloud.

"He knows Ragnar wouldn't give up so easily," Joe remarked. "Could be he figures Sigrid is more vulnerable."

"There's something we've been overlooking," Frank said.

"Which is?" Nancy prodded.

"The culprit must know the Larsens pretty well to be able to play on this Ridder myth," Frank said slowly.

"And if that's the case," Nancy continued,

"he also knows for sure that Ragnar won't be scared off by chess pieces."

"Exactly," Frank said.

"That could mean this Ridder will try something more serious to convince Ragnar," Joe said, his forehead creasing.

Nancy swallowed hard. If Ridder really was a maniac, then Joe's conclusion was a good possibility.

"We'd better get back to work," Nancy said. She stood up and put her hand on Frank's shoulder. "Thanks for telling me about Gillespie. I should warn Bess."

"Don't worry about Bess. I'll keep an eye on her," Joe promised. "She'll be safe."

Nancy waved goodbye and started down the bleachers, taking a different route down from the one she'd come up. Ahead lay the broadcasters' booth and far below Nancy saw the archers heading off the field to be replaced by the track-and-field competitors. As she took the stairs, Nancy thought there was something odd about this section of bleachers.

"Hello!" Looking to her left, Nancy saw Ragnar pounding up the bleachers toward her. Ragnar's feet sounded like hammers on the old wooden seats.

Hammers!

All at once, Nancy realized why this section looked different. She'd seen it from the ground the day before—when there were yellow tapes and barrels warning everyone to stay off. These bleachers were supposed to be replaced.

But now the yellow tapes and warning barrels were gone and the boards hadn't been replaced yet!

"Ragnar, stop!" Nancy hopped down on the next wooden seat. "Don't come any farther—"

Then Nancy heard the sound of wood snapping under her feet. Before she could jump to safety, she was plunging right through the stands. The ground was thirty feet below!

Chapter Eight

AS SHE FELL, Nancy threw out her hands. Her right hand caught the edge of a broken board, and her left arm slid on top of a crossbeam. She gasped in pain as sharp splinters cut into her right hand and left elbow. Glancing down, she watched as debris fluttered past her, tumbling into the shadows below.

As she dangled from the beam, Nancy strengthened her right-hand grip. But she couldn't stop her legs from swinging wildly.

Then she heard the sound of footsteps above. Looking up, she saw Frank and Joe outlined in the sunlight.

"Keep back," she managed to shout. "The boards aren't safe!"

Frank's voice drifted down to her. "Hold on, Nancy! Just keep holding on. We'll get you out of this!"

Astonished, Nancy heard them run off. They were leaving her. The strain on her muscles made her gasp, and she felt as if she'd dislocated her shoulder. The blood was rushing to her feet, and they felt heavy and tingly.

As the minutes passed, Nancy felt herself slipping. Finally, when she knew she couldn't hold on any longer, she heard shouting below. Looking down, Nancy saw Frank, Joe, Ragnar, and several other athletes ducking under the crossbeams.

"Come on, Nancy," Frank said. She saw they had unrolled a large blanket and were holding it tight by the edges. "Pretend we're the fire department."

Nancy's heartbeat doubled as she watched them pull the blanket taut into a safety net. Would it hold her weight?

There wasn't time to worry. She let go of her weak grip and felt herself plummet to the ground. In seconds she had landed squarely in the center of the blanket.

Frank and Joe let out a yell. "You did it!" they shouted.

Ragnar helped Nancy to her feet. "I think

you just won the women's high-drop," he joked. "Are you okay?"

Nancy gulped, then nodded, relieved to be on solid ground again. She looked up at the sunlight streaming in through the hole above. "How far?"

"Thirty feet," Frank murmured, coming over to her. "High enough to break a leg."

Ragnar had folded the blanket and was leading his teammates away. As soon as they were out of earshot, Frank turned back to her.

"You scared the living daylights out of me when I saw you fall through that floor. What happened?" he asked.

Nancy brushed her tangled hair out of her face. "The boards just gave way. But I don't think it was meant for me," she said, giving Frank a serious look.

"Ragnar?" Frank asked.

Nancy nodded. "There were warning barrels there yesterday—I remembered them too late—but now they're gone."

"It makes sense," Joe said in a low voice. "Everybody in the stadium knows that Ragnar runs up and down the bleachers each day."

"Let's take a look." Frank started sifting through the pile of rubble. With a surprised grunt, he lifted a splintered two-by-four from the mound of debris. He scraped one end with his thumb and fresh sawdust fell away.

"No wonder the board broke," he said, handing her the beam.

Nancy looked at it carefully. "Somebody cut the support beams," Joe said from over her shoulder.

Nancy shuddered slightly.

"Get a load of this." Joe picked up a small white figurine. A piece of paper formed a collar around the chess king's neck.

Nancy unwrapped the paper and read the message out loud. " 'When the king falls, the game is over.' " She looked up at Frank and Joe. "It looks like Ridder is back. And this time he means business."

"I think Ragnar should know about this," Frank said. Nancy nodded, and together the three strolled downfield toward the Norwegian team's practice spot.

Ragnar must have noticed them, because he came running over. "Do you feel okay?" he asked Nancy.

"Fine. Ragnar, there's something you should know." Nancy handed him the white king. "I found this near where I fell. There was a note, too," she added.

"What did it say?" Ragnar asked. When Nancy told him, Ragnar cleared his throat softly. "Please, don't tell Sigrid about this. If she finds out that I could have been injured, she'll fall apart."

"Why does Ridder scare Sigrid so much?" Frank asked.

"It's very complicated, Frank," Ragnar said, sighing. "When our parents died, my grandfather got us a nanny named Varmor who used to tell Sigrid all kinds of old folktales. Varmor used to tease Sigrid that unless she was good, Ridder would come and take me away."

"She couldn't have known what kind of effect she was having on Sigrid," Nancy said quietly. "She still thinks it's possible."

Ragnar took a deep breath and set his square jaw. "I'll make sure Sigrid is all right. You just find him. Find whoever is doing this to my sister!"

"The whole family sounds loony to me," Joe said as they walked toward Hewitt's office. They thought the security chief should know about Nancy's recent accident. "Ghosts, old Norwegian legends, a crazy nanny named Varmor," Joe added.

"It doesn't matter if they're nuts or not," Frank said, leading the way. "What matters is that someone knows about this and is playing on it for all it's worth."

Inside the field house they could hear Hewitt's voice as he was shouting to someone.

Nancy, Frank, and Joe walked down the hall and waited in Hewitt's doorway until he motioned them to come in and sit down. He reached over and put the phone's speaker on. Jim Overton's agitated voice rang out.

"You've got to find this guy, Hewitt! What's he going to do next? Grab a rifle and start shooting? It's a miracle Larsen wasn't killed."

"We can handle it," Hewitt said, his voice hoarse. "But I told you earlier, we need off-duty cops put all around the stadium."

"You know we can't do that," Overton shouted. "The minute the press hears about cops swarming all over, we're finished. People won't come near this place. Just tell those detectives of yours to get on the ball!"

"Try to be patient, Jim," Hewitt said calmly. "Nancy and the Hardys are closing in on some suspects. I promise we'll have it all sorted out soon."

"I hope so. For your sake. If this character is still running around loose with spectators in here, I shudder to think what might happen. Keep me posted."

A dial tone told them that Overton had hung up. Hewitt took out his handkerchief and let out a huge sneeze.

"Bless you," Frank said, shaking his head. " 'Closing in'—I like that. Dad said you were a politician."

"Let's get some sun. It might do me some good," Hewitt said, leading the way out of his office.

"That's some cold you've got," Frank said, closing the field house door.

"Actually, it's a sinus infection. I've had them all my life. I moved to Santa Teresa in part because the dry air's good for me."

"Maybe you ought to see a doctor," Nancy suggested. "I bet a good dose of penicillin would clear up your infection."

"I bet it would," Hewitt said with an ironic laugh. "But I'd end up in the hospital with an allergic reaction instead. One drop of penicillin puts me in intensive care."

"I once had a friend with that same problem," Joe began.

At that moment Nancy saw Rosalia Vargas racing toward them.

Ignoring the Hardys and Nancy, Rosalia tugged at Hewitt's elbow. "You've got to hurry," she cried. "It's Sigrid. They sent me for you."

Hewitt gripped the girl by her shoulders. "Rosalia, what is it? What's the matter?"

"I don't know." Rosalia shook her head. "But I'd swear on my grandmother's grave that Sigrid Larsen has gone completely mad!"

Chapter Nine

NANCY FROZE. "Ridder," she said, looking at Frank. He nodded. "Where is she?" Nancy asked.

"At the pool. She was in the middle of practice—" Rosalia began.

"Let's go!" Joe shouted.

Nancy followed Frank and Joe as they took off around the stadium. She dragged Rosalia along, leaving Hewitt standing with his mouth open.

They ran across the parking lot, through the quad, and behind the dorms. Soon they'd reached the outdoor pool.

There Nancy saw Sigrid sitting beside the pool, shaking her head and crying softly. George and Grete were trying to comfort her. Tracy Reynolds stood off to one side, confusion on her face.

"Oh, Nancy," Sigrid cried desperately. "He followed me here. Ridder was here."

Nancy was trying to calm Sigrid and avoid the confused looks from the other competitors, who obviously were wondering what Sigrid was doing talking to a nutritionist about someone named Ridder. Glen Hewitt arrived then, panting from the run.

"I called Dr. Matthews," he said, looking at Sigrid. "Is she okay?"

Nancy nodded. "I think so. Here, Sigrid, sit down." She motioned for Hewitt to sit next to the girl, then took George aside.

"What happened?" she whispered.

George seemed confused. "I'm not sure, Nan. We'd just finished a practice heat, and Sigrid said she was going to put on some sunscreen. When she opened her bag, she screamed."

Nancy's eyes darted to the bag, which Frank Hardy was holding open. "Take a look at this," he said, his features tight with anger.

Glancing inside, Nancy saw four broken chess pieces laid out on a bright green towel. Three white pawns and a white queen.

"There's a note, too." Frank showed her a small slip of paper identical to the one they'd found under the bleachers.

"'Pawns can't protect you, princess,'" Nancy read. "So, Ragnar's the white king, Sigrid's the white queen—"

"And we're the pawns," Frank concluded. "I'd say Ridder has us figured out."

"Sigrid!"

Turning, Nancy and Frank saw a pale-faced Ragnar running toward his sister. He crushed her in a fierce embrace. Then, looking into his sister's eyes, Ragnar must have sensed what had happened. "Not Ridder again?" he asked in a whisper.

Sigrid swallowed hard. Nancy could see she was trying to be brave for her brother, but Ridder's latest attack had taken its toll.

When Dr. Matthews arrived a minute later to examine Sigrid, she quietly let him take her pulse and blood pressure. Ragnar stood by his sister.

Frank took Nancy, George, and Joe aside and pointed to Rosalia, whose face Nancy saw was a blend of eagerness and disappointment.

"Rosalia was pretty eager to convince us that Sigrid had gone crazy," Frank said.

"I'm not surprised," George said. "She was in a big hurry to spread the news."

"George, did you happen to see Rosalia near Sigrid's bag?" Nancy asked.

George shook her head. "Nope. But I was in the pool most of the time." George cast a disapproving look at Rosalia. "You know, she claims she's only in the competition for the publicity, but you should see her face whenever her practice time falls behind Sigrid's or Grete's."

Tracy Reynolds was helping Dr. Matthews with Sigrid. "You should be in bed," the doctor was saying to Sigrid.

She shook her head. Then Ragnar spoke up. "He's right, Sigrid. You've practiced enough for today. Save your strength for the competition."

Silently, Sigrid let her new coach walk her toward the locker room.

Joe nudged his brother. "I'll stick with Sigrid," he said. "Just in case Ridder tries another shot."

"Good idea." Frank nodded. "See if you can find out anything from her. Maybe she saw something no one else did."

"You got it." A slow grin brightened Joe's expression. "This is one assignment I think I'll like."

Frank flashed him an impatient look. "Take it easy, Don Juan. That girl is on the verge of a nervous breakdown. You might push her over the edge."

"Just kidding! See you guys later," he said, trailing Sigrid and Tracy.

Ragnar came over as Joe left. "This has got to stop! If Ridder wants—"

"So the great Ragnar Larsen finally shows up, does he?"

George nudged Nancy. Grete Nordstrom was standing right behind Ragnar, her hands on her trim hips.

"What's your problem, Grete?" Ragnar asked over his shoulder. He didn't bother to turn around.

Grete took a few long strides and stood next to Ragnar. "Where were you when Sigrid needed you?" she snapped.

"What do you mean?" Ragnar's face flushed in anger. "I got here as fast as I could."

Nancy, Frank, George, and Joe listened in embarrassment as Grete went on.

"Sigrid says this isn't the first time she's been threatened," she said harshly. "You should have taken it more seriously. But, no, not Ragnar Larsen. Nothing's going to stand in the way of his winning a gold medal in the decathlon."

Ragnar opened his mouth. Nancy flashed him a warning look. There was no need to break their cover.

"If she were *my* sister, I'd take her home!" Grete went on.

"I doubt that." Ragnar's tone was brittle. "You'd stay here and compete, just like me and

Schweigert and everyone else. Maybe you've forgotten about the All-Scandinavia Swimming Championships last year. I seem to remember your 'broken heart' didn't keep you from competing and winning the—"

"Shut up, Ragnar Larsen!" Grete screamed. "How dare you even mention that?"

"Don't accuse me of not caring about my sister, Grete," Ragnar said quietly. His tone was firm.

"Don't even talk to me!" Grete turned her back on Ragnar and offered Nancy an embarrassed but apologetic smile. "Excuse me, please. I have to report for a rubdown. Since for some reason Sigrid seems to trust you, please tell her that if there's anything I can do . . ."

Nancy put on her professional tone. "I'll do that. She needs rest and a proper diet. That's why I'm here."

Nancy knew that if Sigrid continued to fall apart the way she'd done just then, she and the Hardys wouldn't be able to keep their cover for long.

"Whoever this Ridder is, he's deadly serious about keeping you out of the Games," Frank told Ragnar. "You could have broken your legs back there in the stadium."

Ragnar frowned. "You think this has become more than idle threats now, don't you?"

"I do. Ridder's become dangerous."

"The question remains, why?" Nancy mused.

Looking at Ragnar, Frank asked, "Is there anyone who hates you enough to want to kill you?"

Ragnar hesitated. Too long, to Nancy's mind. "I don't know. Schweigert, maybe. He blames me for his losing in Budapest."

"When did that happen?" Frank asked.

"Last year. I beat him in his best event—the fifteen-hundred-meter race. When I offered to shake hands with him afterward, he turned his back on me and walked off the field without a word."

Nancy wasn't persuaded that Ragnar was convinced Schweigert would hurt him. He seemed to clutch at the name.

"Do you really think Schweigert or anyone would try to kill you because of a race?" Nancy asked.

Ragnar backed off, rubbing his forehead nervously. "I don't know," he said. "I can't really think straight right now. I should check on my sister, make sure she's okay."

George offered to go with him, and together they hurried away, leaving Frank and Nancy to walk silently out of the pool together.

Outside, their silence continued, and Nancy shifted her weight from one foot to the other.

She wondered what to say to Frank as an old, familiar breathlessness came over her. Why did she always feel awkward around Frank Hardy?

"I guess we should get going, huh?" Frank asked finally.

"I suppose." Nancy tried to keep her eyes from Frank's, but she found herself compelled to stare into them.

Frank smiled, then, sensing the awkwardness, too. He muttered in a gravelly voice, "Looks as if it's just you and me, shweetheart."

Nancy laughed out loud. "Frank Hardy, you do a really awful Bogart."

"Joe's the performer, not me." Frank looked a little embarrassed. "But I thought we could do with a little tension breaker."

Nancy gave him a long look. "I guess you're right."

"Well, where do we start investigating these latest attacks?"

Nancy started to speak when she saw Lino Passano storming down the walkway. Muttering to himself, he kicked at a trash basket.

Then he looked up and noticed Nancy and Frank. Leveling his forefinger, he started to yell. "There you are. Stay right there. I want to talk to you." Lino took the last few strides toward Nancy at a full-out run.

"What's the matter, Lino?" Nancy asked.

"Don't play dumb with me, you thief." His face reddening with anger, Lino lunged for Nancy and grabbed at her throat.

His grip closed around Nancy's neck. "You've got ten seconds to tell me where it is, or I'll—"

Chapter Ten

FRANK REACTED in an instant. He pulled Lino's left wrist from Nancy's neck and twisted it sharply, and came up behind him. Grimacing, Lino tried to resist, but before he could make a move, Frank had him locked in a full nelson.

"Settle down," Frank ordered.

"She stole my chess set!" Lino hollered, struggling to break free.

"Cool off, Lino. Nancy didn't steal anything."

"Then why was she so interested in it? And how come she had a piece from it? And what was she doing in my room?"

"I told you, Lino," Nancy explained. "Someone hung that piece in Sigrid Larsen's locker. The other missing piece turned up at the banquet last night."

Lino gritted his teeth. "Right! At your table. And when I came back from the banquet, the whole set was gone."

Frank released his grip. "Just why are you so upset about this chess set, anyway? Don't you think you're overreacting?"

"It was hand-carved in Italy. It belonged to my grandfather, and I take it everywhere." Lino seemed to be calming down a little.

"I'm sorry it's gone," Nancy said. "But I honestly didn't have anything to do with it. I'm even sorrier that some of the pieces have been broken."

"What?" Lino asked.

Frank explained about the broken queen and three pawns.

"I should have known. When I got back to the dorm last night, I found my door open. But I know I locked it. I asked around, but no one saw anything. Then Jeff reminded me that you, Nancy, were in my room earlier, and I remembered how you sneaked out of the dining hall during dinner."

Frank smiled to himself. Lino obviously had a lot invested in finding out who had taken his precious chess set.

"Nancy left the dining hall to try to comfort Sigrid," Frank said.

"That's right," Nancy added.

Their answers didn't seem to make Lino any happier. "When I find out who took it—" he started.

"I wouldn't go off half-cocked again, Lino," Frank advised. "You're likely to get bounced out of the Games."

Lino seemed to take Frank's advice to heart. "You're right. I'm sorry," he mumbled before shoving his hands into his jacket pockets and walking away.

"It's very interesting that a certain chess set that Ridder's been using to make his threats is now missing, don't you think?" Frank asked.

"I was just thinking the same thing, Frank Hardy," Nancy said. She grabbed his arm. "Come on, Glen Hewitt should know about this."

Frank nodded. They turned around and headed back to the field house. "If Lino is Ridder," Frank said as they walked through the stadium gates, "then having his chess set stolen would divert suspicion from him."

"But what if he didn't take it? Then the real Ridder must know we're on to him," Nancy added. "Those pawns he left are pretty telling."

They were walking through the gate on the

far side of the stadium when they heard loud voices coming from the field house. Nancy beat Frank to the building and pushed the door to Hewitt's office open in time to see Dave Gillespie hammering Hewitt's desk with his fist.

"You've no right to pull me in here. I didn't have anything to do with those bleachers collapsing!"

Nancy motioned for Frank to be quiet. Gillespie hadn't seen them yet, and she didn't want him to. Frank nodded.

"Look, Gillespie, I don't have to put up with this, you know," Hewitt said. "If you keep playing dumb, I'll let the local police take over. Either way, I'm going to find out where you went after the banquet last night."

Dave's shoulders slumped, and he dropped into the chair across from Hewitt's desk. "I walked Bess Marvin back to her dorm," he said.

Hewitt checked in a notebook on his desk. "Bess says you dropped her off at midnight, but the head of your dorm says he didn't see you come back until three. Where were you in the meantime?"

"I went for a walk, okay?" Dave challenged.

"You'll swear to that?" Hewitt met his challenge.

Gillespie jumped out of his chair. "Look,

what's going on here?" he asked. "Another frame job? I didn't have anything more to do with those bleachers than I did with Juan Valverde dying. Which adds up to exactly nothing!"

Hewitt stood up slowly and straightened his tie. "I've got a case of sabotage. I have a motive for you, and you have no alibi for last night. If I were you, kid, I'd talk to that expensive lawyer your father hired two years ago."

Nancy watched as Dave surged forward, his fist raised. Then, obviously thinking better of it, he lowered his fist, pounding the desk again. "You don't scare me. If you've got something, take me to the cops and have me charged. If not, get off my back!" he yelled.

Dave turned around and stormed out of the office. Frank and Nancy neatly sidestepped him as they slid into the office.

"What was that all about?" Nancy asked.

"Routine investigation." Hewitt sank back into his chair. "After your accident today, I decided to talk to anyone who didn't have an alibi for all of last night. Anyone who could have sneaked in and sawed those crossbeams. And Dave Gillespie seems to have taken offense at being questioned."

"He's not the only one without an alibi, is he?" Nancy asked.

"Unfortunately, no." Hewitt took out his

handkerchief and blew his nose. "I've got two other suspects. The coordinator at Banning told me that she saw Rosalia Vargas sneaking out of the dorm after midnight."

"And you talked to her?" Frank asked.

Hewitt nodded, wiping his nose again. "I tried to. She wouldn't tell me a word about where she went or what time she got back."

"You said you had another suspect," Nancy said. "Who?"

"Jeff Cannon. He was more than a little vague about where he went last night after the banquet. Jumpy as a cat, too," Hewitt added.

"Well, well—" Frank murmured, glancing at Nancy.

Hewitt must have noticed their exchange, because he looked at them expectantly. "What have you got?" he asked.

"It's probably nothing." Frank hesitated. "But the chess set that Ridder's been taking his pieces from is gone."

"What? I think you should tell me what's going on." Hewitt motioned them to sit down. "And you'd better start from the beginning."

Joe Hardy stretched his long, denim-clad legs, trying to get comfortable. The desk chair bit into his back. Grimacing, he shifted position and impatiently flipped through a sports magazine.

Across the room, Sigrid lay sleeping, her

blond hair spilling across the pillow, her face calm and serene.

As Joe watched, she stirred. Her blue eyes fluttered open. She took one look at Joe and let out a startled gasp.

Joe stood up slowly, smiled, and raised his hands, palms forward. "It's okay, Sigrid. I'm one of the good guys," he joked. "See? No chess pieces up my sleeve."

"You're one of the detectives, aren't you?" Sigrid said, burrowing deeper into the bed.

Joe nodded.

"What exactly were you investigating sitting here in my bedroom?" Sigrid stuck her chin out from under the blanket.

This wasn't going to be easy, Joe thought. Sigrid obviously didn't take to waking up with a stranger in her room. "Frank *ordered* me to stand guard," he said. "He was afraid Ridder might try something while you were alone."

Sigrid's indignant expression faded and she managed to smile. "I'm sorry. I should thank you, not question you. I was taken aback, that's all."

"That's okay. I understand. How are you feeling?"

"Groggy." Sigrid pushed her hair back from her forehead. "Have I been asleep long?"

"Six hours. They'll be serving dinner soon," Frank said.

A dimple appeared at the corner of Sigrid's

smile. "You've been sitting here with me for the past six hours? And I don't even know your name." She blushed.

"Joe Hardy. Ace detective. Defender of the weak. Walloper of the wicked. Prince of Bayport. Strong, loyal, lovable, and devastatingly handsome."

Sigrid stopped laughing for a second to breathe.

Joe took her hand and squeezed it reassuringly. "Can I ask you a question or two?"

Sigrid nodded quickly.

"Nancy told me about Ridder," he said, turning serious. "Other than telling her and George, have you mentioned the story to anyone else?"

"No—at least I don't think so." Sigrid's face tensed. "At first, I didn't even think of it myself. But after the chess piece appeared in my locker, I knew it had to be Ridder."

"Would anyone else on the Norwegian team know about Ridder?" Joe asked.

"Of course." Sigrid smiled again. "The story's even told as far away as Finland." Her lips puckered. "I just realized. Grete would know about it."

"Grete Nordstrom?" Joe asked excitedly. A real suspect at last?

"Yes," Sigrid answered. "She and Ragnar used to be—pretty close."

"How close is 'pretty close,' Sigrid?"

Frowning, Sigrid lowered her gaze. "Joe, I'd rather not talk about it. Grete is my friend, and it's not easy to talk about what happened between her and my brother."

Joe patted Sigrid's wrist. "Sure, kid." He made a mental note to ask Frank and Nancy what they knew about Grete and Ragnar the next time he saw them. Then he flashed Sigrid his best smile. "Let's talk about dinner instead. How about you and I go to a cozy Mexican restaurant? I hear there are some great ones in town."

"I've never had Mexican food before," Sigrid said. "It sounds like fun, though."

"Then it's settled. While everyone else is eating the same old boring dining hall food, we're going to be feasting on shrimp, guacamole, and nachos! Let's go!"

"Bess, that's ice cream," Nancy warned.

"I know." Bess greedily stuck her spoon into a mound of creamy pistachio after eating a large dinner. "I don't have to worry about dieting anymore. I worked out with Dave and the guys yesterday and today—"

"You're working out!" Nancy laughed.

"Sure! There isn't much to do after I drag the ice chest out, so the team invited me to work out with them. Dave even showed me these really great aerobic exercises. I feel as if I've lost two pounds already!"

Nancy thought again about Dave Gillespie. Should she warn Bess away from him? She didn't want her friend getting involved with a suspect, especially one with Dave's past.

Bess dropped her spoon. "I'm telling you, Nancy, this is the best job ever!"

"Just don't forget the real reason we're here, Bess." Nancy gave her friend a good hard look. "The Games open the day after tomorrow, and we're no closer to finding Ridder than we were when we got here."

"I know, Nancy, and I'm sorry I haven't been able to help more. But from my end, nothing too suspicious has been going on."

"I understand, Bess." Nancy hesitated. In the end, though, she found she couldn't tell Bess about Dave's possible involvement with Juan Valverde's death. There was no proof.

"But I'm keeping my eyes and ears open," Bess said, grinning at Dave across the dining hall.

"You should be careful, too, you know," Nancy said, trying to warn her.

"Oh, I don't need to worry with Dave around—speaking of terrific guys." Bess smiled impishly, then tilted her head toward George and Ragnar.

Turning around in her chair, Nancy watched

Ragnar and George laughing together. Ragnar put his arm around George's shoulders and led her off toward the gardens that ran beside the dining hall.

Nancy checked her watch—eight-fifteen. They had lingered after dinner for an hour. "Be right back," Nancy whispered to Bess.

George is probably going to kill me for this, Nancy thought as she slipped outside, but it wasn't safe for Ragnar to be wandering around the campus in the gathering darkness. Even with George to protect him, Nancy thought with a laugh.

The cool California dusk enveloped Nancy. As she made her way along the cinder-block wall, the soft light from the dining hall faded and Nancy was hidden in dark shadows from well-trimmed shrubbery and trees.

Nancy listened carefully. Palm fronds rustled over her head. A lawn sprinkler whirred softly. Then Ragnar's singsong lilt floated out of the dark.

"You were going to tell me about that bike race you won."

Nancy heard George laugh. "There's not much to tell, Ragnar. It was a women's three-thousand-meter individual race. . . ."

As George went on, Nancy tiptoed closer to where George's voice was coming from. Suddenly her voice stopped.

Glancing around a shrub, Nancy saw why. George and Ragnar were in each other's arms, their lips joined in a tender kiss.

Nancy ducked down behind the bush. She was about to go back to the dining hall when the noise of a branch breaking stopped her short. One glance over a nearby clump of bushes told her someone else was hiding in the shadow. The moon slid out from under a bank of clouds, and the light was dazzling as it gleamed on something in the bushes. The small branches quivered.

Nancy was heading for the bushes when a gloved fist rose above the shrub. She recognized the long slender object in its grasp. A javelin!

"George!" Nancy shouted. She turned and tried to make a diving leap to save George and Ragnar.

But she was too late! Above her head, Nancy saw the javelin cut through the air, right on target for Ragnar and George!

Chapter Eleven

NANCY'S CRY got their attention. In the semidarkness, she watched Ragnar push George to the ground. With a sharp noise, the javelin pierced a nearby tree.

"What—" Nancy saw George crawling out from under Ragnar. "You could have hurt me," Nancy heard her say.

"Not as much as this." Ragnar was pointing to the javelin as Nancy ran over to them.

"Are you okay?" Nancy asked breathlessly.

"We're fine, Nan. But what just happened?" George was still on the ground and was rubbing her shoulder where Ragnar had landed on her.

"I'll tell you in a minute." Satisfied that George and Ragnar were all right, Nancy plunged into the shrubbery. Branches rustled and snapped, outlining the killer's escape route.

Nancy continued to make her way along the path leading to the nearby parking lot. Then she felt something pull at her ankle. She tripped and threw out her hands to protect herself as the ground rushed up to meet her.

"Rats!" she said to herself. She pulled herself up off the ground and was brushing the hair from her eyes when nearby she heard an engine roar to life. A dark van, running without lights, squealed out of the parking lot, heading for the main exit.

Nancy grimaced in disgust. She'd lost him.

She shook her head and headed back up the path. George and Ragnar were coming toward her. Ragnar held the javelin and they both looked shaken.

"I don't know what would have happened if you hadn't come along when you did," George murmured softly to her.

"I'm not sorry now that I followed you," Nancy said with a grim smile. "But I think the three of us should report this to Glen Hewitt right away."

Ragnar and George nodded. The three of them walked slowly away from the rectangles of light from the dining hall and toward the darkened stadium.

"What's so strange," Ragnar said after a minute, "is that this is an official Games javelin, not some simple practice model." He looked it over carefully. "And it's practically brand-new."

"Not to mention the fact that whoever did it is a good shot," Nancy added, taking the javelin from Ragnar. "He was in the bushes all the time, watching you both and taking careful aim."

"You don't think it was Dave Gillespie, do you?" George asked.

Nancy was quiet. The same thought had crossed her mind.

"Gillespie?" Ragnar asked. He looked genuinely shocked. "Why would he want to kill me?"

"To make sure he wins the decathlon," Nancy answered.

"If you had said Schweigert, I might have believed you." Ragnar shook his head. "But Gillespie? I don't think so."

Nancy stood still. "Keep this to yourself, Ragnar, but the local police think Dave may have been responsible for the death of his number one rival in high school."

Ragnar exploded. "What's going on here? How could they let someone like that compete?"

"They couldn't prove anything," Nancy said quietly. Then she went on, the javelin resting on her shoulder. "But let's not assume it's Dave. The same motive could apply to your other rivals. Lino seems a little irrational, to say the least."

George looked thoughtful. "It's got to be one of the guys, right?"

"Not necessarily, George. There are girls who could throw the javelin just as well—"

He cut himself short, as if realizing he'd said too much. In the darkness Nancy thought she saw a worried frown crease his handsome face.

Glen Hewitt wasn't in his office, but the night supervisor at Games security told them he'd relay the message first thing in the morning. By that time George was her irrepressible self again, and on the way back to the dorm she even joked about the grass stains on her dress. After kissing Ragnar good night, George went into the building. Nancy lingered in the doorway for a moment.

"I need to ask you something, Ragnar," she said quietly. She put her hand on his arm. "You're protecting Grete, aren't you?"

His eyes flickered. "Why do you—"

"I know that you and Grete are old—friends," Nancy answered. "How would Grete do at throwing a javelin?"

Ragnar's proud shoulders drooped. He was

quiet for so long, Nancy was sure he wasn't going to answer her. She waited.

"She used to compete before concentrating exclusively on swimming," Ragnar said finally.

"Do you think Grete Nordstrom would want to hurt you, even kill you?" Nancy asked gently.

Sadness softened the hard line of Ragnar's mouth. With his hands in his pockets, he stared at the dark sky overhead. "Grete and I met while training for a competition. We fell in love. When the competition ended, she expected me to follow her back to Stockholm. She even told her friends we were going to get married."

"What happened?" Nancy prodded.

Ragnar rubbed his eyes and looked down at his feet. "I wasn't ready, I thought we were too young. I broke it off. Grete's very proud, and I suppose I ended up humiliating her. She's not the type to forget something like that."

Nancy was quiet. She remembered her first meeting with Grete and the girl's sharp remarks about Ragnar. Later, Grete had yelled at Ragnar after Sigrid had found those four chess pieces in her gym bag. Obviously, Grete hadn't taken the breakup lightly. But did she hate Ragnar enough to kill him? Also, she seemed to be happy with Lino now.

Ragnar stepped around Nancy and opened the door for her. "Please," he said, looking into her eyes. "Don't mention what happened tonight to Sigrid. She's upset enough as it is."

"I'll make sure she doesn't find out," Nancy reassured him. "Try not to worry too much. We'll figure this out. Good night." Nancy walked into the lobby and turned back to see Ragnar still holding the door, lost in thought.

Sunlight bounced off the stainless steel countertops as Nancy hurried into the dining hall the next morning. She squinted her eyes against the brightness. Bess's cheerful voice rang out. "Over here, Nancy!"

Crossing the crowded room, Nancy saw Bess, George, Ragnar, and Sigrid sitting around a circular table. Mild shadows darkened the delicate skin under Sigrid's eyes, but other than that she seemed relatively calm.

"Good morning!" Grinning, Ragnar pointed to an empty chair. "Have a seat." From his mood, Nancy guessed he was pretending that nothing had happened the night before.

Nancy took a quick look at the long breakfast line. "Let me get something to eat and I'll join you."

Frank Hardy's cheerful voice rang out behind her. "I saved you the trouble," he said, setting a breakfast tray on the table in front of her. Joe came over a moment later, carrying a plate heaped high with ham and eggs.

Looking at the plate Frank had gotten for her, Nancy laughed. "Bacon, fried eggs, hash browns, and english muffins. You even remembered what I ordered at the Winslow Hotel!"

Frank sat down and unfolded his napkin. "It was a memorable case, Nancy."

"Did you hear?" Ragnar asked. "The Games committee has given us the day off to rest up for tomorrow's opening day. It's traditional that they give us this day off, but they never announce it until the morning. Not even my coach can make me practice."

Sigrid smiled. "Ragnar and I want to see a little more of California."

"And Tracy told us about a really great bike tour through the Tularosa Mountains," George added.

"So we're going to rent bikes. Are you in?" Frank asked.

"You bet," Nancy said. The athletes might have the day, but did Ridder? Ragnar and Sigrid would still need protection.

Ragnar stretched in his chair. "Well, hurry up and eat. We've got a big day ahead of us."

Bike wheels whirred as Nancy guided her ten-speed around a long bend. Mountain sunshine basted her from helmet to sneakers. Her calf muscles strained with fatigue.

Up ahead, the two-lane road climbed upward, meeting the narrow cleft of the next pass. Off to the right, the ponderosa-clad slopes of a faraway peak split the azure sky. George and Ragnar were out in front, determinedly setting the pace. Joe and Sigrid pedaled along just behind them, carrying on an energetic conversation. Frank cruised along on Nancy's right.

As the slope steepened, Nancy heard Bess's rasping breaths behind her. Peering over her shoulder, Nancy saw Bess wobbling on her bike, her flushed face wet with sweat.

"Naaanncy—" Bess wailed in a pitiful tone.

"You can do it, Bess. We're almost to the top."

"I'll never make it," Bess moaned.

Weber Pass was the halfway point on their trip. From there they had a breathtaking view of the entire area—a stunning landscape of brown hills, rugged peaks, and the far-off shimmer of the ocean. They all got off their bikes to take in the sight.

Nancy stretched out beneath a pine tree, with Bess and Frank on either side of her. While they sipped from their water bottles, Nancy watched Joe and Sigrid stroll along the top of the bluff.

"They seem to be getting along pretty well," Nancy said to Frank with a smile.

"Almost as well as George and Ragnar,"

Frank added, pointing to where the two sat on a nearby boulder, holding hands.

"I hate to break the spell, but we should be going if we want to get back before lunch," Nancy said, standing. "Come on, Bess." She offered her friend a hand.

Bess groaned. "Can't you send a cab for me?"

Taking Bess's hand, Nancy hauled her to her feet. "It's all downhill from here. Piece of cake."

"Okay, okay. I think I can, I think I can." Bess tried to laugh as she got back on her bike. "But I'm not promising anything."

Leaving the pass, the friends biked back to the coast on a narrow mountain road running along the rim of a canyon. Nancy and Frank brought up the rear, coasting along the shoulder and looking down into the gorge.

Frank whistled softly. "That's some drop. Two hundred feet at least."

"I think I'll keep my distance, thanks!" Nancy blinked as the roadside reflectors caught the sun's glare. She steered her bike away from the guardrail, and Frank moved ahead of her. Then she heard a louder *whish* over the whisper of her spokes and turned to glance over her shoulder.

A dark blue van was hurtling downhill, its engine unusually quiet. She suddenly realized that the driver must be coasting in neutral. And he was bearing down on them fast!

Taking a look inside the van, Nancy saw the driver was wearing a black hood that completely shadowed his face.

Ridder!

In a second he had passed them all and was turning the van to the right. The van's bumper swung ominously toward Ragnar, who was moving so fast he couldn't hear the car right behind him.

Nancy threw her bike out of gear, her speed doubled. She raced past Frank, then Joe and Sigrid, who shouted after her.

As she caught up with Ridder, Nancy threw out her hand to grab the van's passenger door.

Startled, the hooded driver swerved, and Nancy weaved to avoid him. Tires howled on the asphalt. Nancy's bike skidded on loose gravel. She lost control, veering helplessly toward the guard rail. Her bike hit the metal barrier, and she was catapulted off.

In a flash she was hurtling over the cliff's edge!

Chapter Twelve

As Nancy flew into the air she glimpsed with horror the distant canyon floor.

Then something entered her field of vision—a slim upright reflector post, jutting up from the edge of the bluff.

Twisting her body in midair, Nancy made a frantic grab for the thin aluminum post. It bent under her weight and sagged with an awful creaking sound, but it stayed anchored.

With her heart in her mouth, Nancy swayed back and forth. Looking down, she saw a rocky streambed far below.

"Nancy, give me your hand!"

Peering, Nancy saw Frank inching his way face forward over the cliff edge. Joe and Ragnar were bracing his legs. Bess, George, and Sigrid looked on anxiously.

Nancy held on to the pole firmly with her right hand while she clawed her left one up to meet Frank's. Frank's firm grip closed around her wrist.

"Got you!" He pulled her up, and within minutes she was back on safe ground again. Her body trembled from the sudden adrenaline rush, and her mouth felt like cotton.

"What happened?" Sigrid asked, wide-eyed.

"That guy in the van tried to run us off the road." Nancy turned to the Hardys. "Did you see anything?"

Frank nodded grimly. "I managed to get a look. It was a late-model van, navy blue, with a logo on the side. 'White Shield Truck Rental.' "

"It had California plates," Joe added. "But the numbers were covered with fresh mud. He was going too fast to see, anyway."

"I got a look at the driver," Nancy said, still breathing roughly. "But I couldn't tell if it was a man or a woman. Whoever it was had on a black hood—"

"Ridder!" Sigrid went white. "That's what he wore in Oslo the night he killed the traitor's son—"

Ragnar grabbed his sister by the arms. "Sigrid, that was hundreds of years ago. It couldn't have been—"

"It was!" Sigrid insisted, trembling. "He came for us again."

Nancy touched Sigrid's shoulder gently. "Think for a minute, Sigrid. How did this medieval Norwegian Ridder become so familiar with California?"

Sigrid looked at her blankly.

"And why would a ghost bother to come after us in a van?" she added. "Whoever is doing this is human. Somebody who knows the Ridder legend—"

"And who knows his way around Tularosa County. He knew just what roads to take to find us." Shading his eyes, Frank studied the road behind them. "He timed the attack perfectly. Rolled down the slope in neutral, gunned the engine, tried to hit Ragnar, then took off down the mountain."

Finally Sigrid seemed to understand. "You're right, of course," she said quietly. "It must be a real person."

Casting a worried glance at Sigrid, Joe turned to Nancy. "Are you sure he was after Ragnar this time?" he asked.

Nancy nodded. "Positive. I saw the whole thing."

Frank picked up the mangled remains of

Nancy's ten-speed. "You're not getting far on this. Come on, you can ride back to Santa Teresa on my handlebars."

"Frank Hardy, I haven't ridden on anybody's handlebars since I was ten." Nancy couldn't keep the grin off her face.

"It's a skill you never forget." Frank tilted his head invitingly. "Let's go."

They arrived back on campus shortly before noon. Frank and Joe headed downtown to run their description of Ridder's van past the Santa Teresa police. After seeing Sigrid safely to the dorm and asking George and Bess to keep the girl company, Nancy made her way to the security office.

As she entered the stadium, Nancy heard a man's voice call her name. She looked up to see Jim Overton climbing down from the nearby bleachers.

"What's the latest on the case?" he asked.

Nancy briefly described Ridder's attack up in the mountains. As she spoke, the worry lines in Overton's face deepened.

"Nancy, you people have to do better than that. What if Ridder tries to kill them during the Parade of Athletes tomorrow? In front of millions of people watching the show on TV? Can you imagine the impact on the Games?"

Nancy looked at him skeptically. It occurred to her that Overton cared more about gate receipts than athletes. Don't be naive, she told herself, it's up to him to worry about how the Games come off, and that includes preventing some killer in black cape and hood from going crazy.

"Maybe you can help us," Nancy said finally. "Were you here all morning?"

Overton nodded curtly. "Sure I was. It's my job to be around. I was helping the TV network set up. Why?"

"Did you see any of the following people this morning?" Nancy asked, ignoring his question and counting off on her fingers. "Dave Gillespie, Kurt Schweigert, Lino Passano, Grete Nordstrom."

Overton's mouth puckered. "I think the boys went into town. But I did see Grete. She said she was on her way to Sea Gate Mall with Rosalia Vargas."

"But you didn't see Rosalia?" Nancy asked.

Overton shook his head briskly. "Why all these questions? Why not try to figure out who's behind this?"

"I'm trying," Nancy said. She just managed to keep the edge out of her voice. "And believe me, as soon as I do, you'll be the first to know."

"Good," Overton said with finality. "Now I've got to get back to work. Listen, I'm sorry to be so short with you, but this whole situation makes me look really bad. I hope you understand." With that, he walked away.

Nancy followed him with her eyes, shook her head and continued on her way to Glen Hewitt's office. After reporting what had happened, Nancy was making her way through the stadium when she ran into Frank and Joe. "Find anything?" she asked, smiling.

"Frank and I just had an interesting chat with the police," Joe said decisively. "Someone broke into the White Shield Truck Rental lot late last night and stole a dark van."

"The same one that practically ran us all down," Nancy concluded. "Did they find the van?"

"Sure did," Frank said. "Unfortunately, the inside was wiped clean: no prints, nothing."

"So much for that clue," Nancy said with a sigh.

That afternoon Nancy padded in thongs across the white sands of the university's private beach. Whitecaps tumbled out of the ocean and broke on the shore. Nancy looked up at two squawking gulls hovering over a vendor's stand.

The beach trip had been Bess's idea, and Nancy had to admit that it was a good one. Sigrid was relaxing on a beach towel, and Nancy saw that she looked much less worried than she had in days. Until they found Ridder, the best Nancy could do would be to keep Sigrid calm for the competition.

"Did you call Ned?" Sigrid asked when Nancy was in earshot.

"He'll be here after work," Nancy said. She sat down next to Sigrid on her towel. Grete Nordstrom and Tracy Reynolds were stretched out sunning not far from them. "How are you feeling?" Nancy asked Sigrid.

"Better." Her smile was timid. "I'm glad you talked me into coming. Everyone's having so much fun. Usually we don't get a chance to relax with one another like this."

Nancy looked around to see an impromptu Frisbee game that Joe, Bess, Dave, Lino, and Kurt were waging along the water's edge. Dave and Lino were showing off, hurling the Frisbee discus-style. Kurt leapt five feet in the air to snatch the Frisbee away from Joe.

"Disgusting," Nancy heard Grete say. Then she realized what the girl was talking about. George and Ragnar were playing in the waves, splashing each other. Before Nancy could defend her friend, Rosalia came running up to them with a volleyball tucked under her arm.

"I'm challenging you to a game, Sigrid," she said, dark eyes flashing. "My team against Ragnar and your friends."

Sigrid stood up and grinned. "And just who's on your team?"

"I am," Tracy said, then pointed to Grete. "And she just volunteered."

Rosalia nodded in the direction of Dave,

Lino, and Kurt. "Those three will make a pretty good attack line."

Soon, they'd drawn up teams. Even Jim Overton was enlisted to play. He had been sitting with Ragnar—in a moment of relaxation as he told them—when they convinced him to join. Nancy found herself on the attack line for her team, along with Joe and George. An eager Kurt grinned at them through the net mesh. Ragnar, Frank, and Overton formed the backline for their team. Bess gratefully took refuge in the tall referee's chair.

Sigrid's powerful serve started a flurry of activity on Rosalia's team, which moved with lightning speed. In the first point alone, Nancy spent all her time blocking the determined spikes of Kurt and Grete.

Forty minutes into the game, the score was tied at eleven-eleven. Sigrid's team needed four more points to win. Frank served, sending the ball deep into Rosalia's rear court. Dave got under it, jumped up and gave it a two-armed slam.

The ball flew at the white tape on top of the net mesh. Nancy watched as both George and Grete went for it, their arms tangled at the top of the net. The ball skidded out of bounds. George landed in a heap on the sand.

"Foul!" Ragnar cried.

"It was not," Grete snapped. "It's not my fault if your *girlfriend's* too clumsy."

Ragnar helped George to her feet, brushing the sand off her. "You kneed her on purpose, Grete," he said.

"I did not!" Grete shouted.

"I saw you," Ragnar said coldly. "Either play fair or quit."

Fuming, Grete picked up the ball and threw it at him. "I'll take the second choice." She stormed off. Tracy followed her and tried to persuade her to come back, but it was useless. The game was over.

After putting his glasses back on, Kurt ducked under the net and offered to shake hands. "It was fun while it lasted, anyway," he said to Nancy.

Nancy shook his hand. "Good game, Kurt."

"You know, for people who claim not to be athletes, you three are in very good shape." Then he pointed to Overton. "And you're not bad yourself, Mr. Overton."

Overton mopped his sweating face with a towel. "It's all a matter of conditioning, Kurt. Let's see if you're this fit when you're my age. Well, time to get back to work. See you guys later," he said, walking off.

Kurt waved goodbye and ran down to the water to catch up with Lino.

Nancy, Frank, and Joe joined the Larsens and walked over to where Ragnar had been sitting. "Maybe I should talk to Grete," Sigrid said, casting a glance up the beach.

Ragnar made a face. "Don't waste your time. When Grete's in one of these moods, nothing does any good. Let Lino talk to her." He flashed George an apologetic look. "I'm sorry she had to ruin the game, though."

"Me, too," George said bravely.

With a weary groan, Ragnar leaned back on his towel. "I'm not going to worry about it, and none of you should either." He stretched out his legs and rested his head in his hands.

Suddenly, Nancy saw Ragnar flinch his right leg. He sat up with a jolt, then let out a cry.

"What's wrong, Ragnar?" George asked.

Nancy watched as Ragnar gripped his leg. Before he could answer, Nancy realized what had made Ragnar act so strangely.

From between the fingers holding his thigh, Nancy saw a stream of blood gushing from Ragnar's leg!

Chapter Thirteen

"I'M CUT!" RAGNAR SHOUTED, clamping his hand over the wound and scooting free of his bloody, shredded towel.

Nancy reacted in an instant. She grabbed the towel she was lying on and darted to Ragnar. Frank and Joe were also there.

"I'll keep my hand above the cut," Frank told Nancy. Joe was already tearing up Nancy's towel into strips. Nancy took the pieces and used them to tie a makeshift tourniquet.

Gasping, Sigrid hurried forward to help, but Nancy held her back. "Hold it, Sigrid. Let's have no more injuries."

Frank was pulling back the torn towel that Ragnar had been sitting on. "Ragnar must have cut himself on broken glass or something metal. It sure cut up this towel," he explained when Nancy looked at him quizzically. He asked George to get a doctor.

Working in tandem, Nancy and Frank slowly sifted their fingers through the sand, while Joe cleaned Ragnar's wound. One by one, jagged shards of bottle green glass emerged. Nancy put them in a little pile off to one side.

Then Nancy felt her fingers make contact with something smooth and plastic. She pulled it out of the loose sand. Its horse's head seemed to sneer at her. Another black knight! Not from Lino's set, but delivering the same message.

Frank's eyes narrowed grimly. "This wasn't an accident," he said.

Nancy nodded. "Ridder again."

Sigrid must have overheard them. Nancy watched as she hugged her brother desperately, and spoke to him in a defeated whisper. "He won't leave us alone, will he?" Tears glimmered in her glacial blue eyes. "Who, Ragnar? Who could possibly hate us so much?"

"I'm not sure." Ashen faced, Ragnar tried to get up. Sigrid put her arm around his waist and helped him stand. For the first time, Nancy saw him looking genuinely afraid.

"I don't understand," he said quietly. "How does he do it? How does he always know where to find us? How did he get onto this beach? It's private."

"I don't know, Ragnar," Nancy answered. "But here comes George and two medics. They'll take you to the doctor. We'll let you know if we find out anything," Nancy said as Ragnar got onto the stretcher and was carried away with George and Sigrid following behind.

"I'll go with them, Nancy," Bess spoke up. "They look like they could use the company," she whispered.

"Thanks, Bess," Nancy said.

Nancy knelt, picked up a green glass shard, and held it up to the sunlight.

Frank squatted next to her. "What are you thinking, Nancy?"

"How *did* Ridder get onto the university's private beach? He couldn't have just sneaked in here. Not past the security checks."

Frank followed her train of thought. "This is definite now. He's one of us. One of the group we were playing with. No one else was near this area."

Joe nodded. His gaze wandered down to the water where Lino, Grete, and Kurt were throwing around the Frisbee. They seemed to be oblivious to what had happened to Ragnar. "What else do we know?"

"It had to be someone who saw Ragnar lie

down on that towel earlier, then he or she planted the broken glass and the chess piece. And whoever did it probably bought the bottle the broken glass came from at that stand over there."

Frank, Joe, and Nancy approached the vendor's stand. An overweight, sunburned man in a white paper cap and Golden State University T-shirt nodded a greeting. "What'll you have, kids?"

Nancy spied a case of Sierra Cola beside the refrigerator. The long-necked bottles were the same emerald shade as the broken glass. She nudged Frank, then tilted her chin in that direction.

Frank reached for his wallet. "Two Sierras, please."

Joe joined in. "Make that three, please. The sun's a fryolator today."

"I'll bet you've had a lot of business today seeing as it's so hot," Nancy said nonchalantly.

"Sure have! I've gone through four cases of Sierras already. In fact, one kid had three in an hour."

"Oh, really? Who?" Nancy couldn't keep the growing excitement out of her voice.

"That guy with the glasses." The vendor pointed at Kurt Schweigert, who was standing ankle-deep in the surf. As Nancy and the Hardys watched, he took a long swig from a green Sierra bottle.

"Let's go!" Frank said excitedly.

On their way down to Kurt, they mapped out their strategy.

"Hey, Kurt, do you ever play chess?" Joe asked innocently.

"Sometimes." Kurt looked at them in mild curiosity. "Why do you ask?"

Nancy held up the chess piece. "We were wondering if this belonged to you?"

Fingering it, Kurt made a face and shook his head. "No, it's not mine. Besides, I left my chess set back home in Stuttgart."

"Didn't you just drink a Sierra Cola?" asked Nancy.

She studied the German boy's face, waiting for his answer. If he denied it or lied about it, then that would make him a prime suspect.

"Actually, I bought two," Kurt said candidly. "Grete gave me some money and asked me to buy them for her. Why do you ask?"

"No reason. Just curious."

Grete! She had as strong a motive as Kurt, Nancy realized. And since she was Ragnar's old girlfriend, she probably knew all about his rivalry with the German athlete. Had Grete set that booby trap, hoping to frame Kurt?

Nancy beckoned Frank and Joe with a nod of her head and pointed with her eyes toward where Grete was walking along the beach with Lino. "Thanks," she said. Frank walked ahead of his brother and Nancy toward the Swedish girl.

"Excuse me." Kurt shouted after them. "But what is this all about?"

"We'll explain it to you later!" Joe hollered over his shoulder.

Turning to Nancy and Joe, Frank whispered, "I'll take the lead on this. I'm with Games security. Joe—Nancy—watch their reactions, okay?"

Nancy nodded eagerly.

Frank tapped Grete on the shoulder. She gave him a guarded look. "Yes?"

"You asked Kurt to buy you two bottles of Sierra Cola," Frank said matter-of-factly.

"Yes . . ." Grete's cool gaze raked him from forehead to sandals. "So?"

"Someone put broken glass beside Ragnar's towel. He could have been seriously hurt," Frank replied evenly. "We believe that glass came from a Sierra Cola bottle. What did you do with those bottles Kurt bought for you?"

Grete's eyes were like pale blue fire. "Are you implying that I—"

"It's only a friendly question, Grete."

She folded her arms decisively. "I don't think I will answer that."

"Why not?" Joe asked.

"Because I resent being called a criminal!" Grete's reaction was more interesting than Nancy had thought it would be.

"No one's calling you a criminal, Grete," Frank assured her. "I'm just trying to find out if someone in our group played a dirty trick on Ragnar."

Lino's voice rang out behind them. "She can't show you the bottles."

Frank looked over his shoulder. "Why not?"

"Because somebody took them."

"What?" Joe asked.

Lino knelt and patted a red-and-white cooler. "Grete asked me to put them in my chest. When I opened it up to get them to drink, they were both gone!" He made a rueful face. "I'm telling you—America is full of thieves!"

Frank looked in frustration at Grete. "You could have told me that the first time."

"I don't have to tell Ragnar Larsen's friend *anything!"* she snapped. Picking up a Frisbee, she marched away in anger.

Nancy shrugged her shoulders when Frank cast a glance at her. "Another dead end," she said matter-of-factly.

"There have been too many of them in this case," Frank said.

"You said it, brother," Joe added. "Come on, let's pack up and get out of here. I have a bad taste in my mouth, and I don't think it's salt. Meet you in the parking lot," he said.

"Okay." Frank nodded.

"Lino and Grete could be lying," Nancy remarked after she and Frank picked up their towels and the glass shards and headed for the lot.

"Or Kurt," Frank said.

Nancy looked at the glass fragments lying in Frank's towel. "Oh, well, maybe there are fingerprints."

"Hewitt's got a fingerprint kit in his office," said Frank. "We can dust them there."

"What are we waiting for then? Let's go!" Nancy said enthusiastically.

"That's the Nancy Drew I know!"

"You know, so far, Ridder's been able to stay two steps ahead of us, and—owww!"

Nancy grimaced and stopped short. She kneaded the muscles of her left thigh.

"What's the matter?" asked Frank.

"I must have pulled a muscle falling from my bike this morning."

"Lean on me." Frank put a friendly arm around Nancy. "We can have Doc Matthews take a look at it, if you want."

Nancy leaned against Frank's shoulder as she walked gingerly over the crest of the sand dunes and down the ridge. Nancy spotted a familiar dark-haired guy striding across the parking lot.

"Ned!" she blurted out.

Embarrassment painted Nancy's face a rich crimson. She hurriedly freed herself of Frank's arm. But the damage was already done.

Ned Nickerson stopped short, his handsome face troubled.

"I didn't expect you until later, Ned," Nancy said.

"Obviously not." A muscle ticked in Ned's jaw. "If you're heading back to the dorm, I'll give you a ride."

Nancy nearly accepted the offer. Then she remembered those glass fragments. She had to check them out. There was no time to lose. Ridder's next attempt on the Larsens might be fatal!

"Thanks, Ned, but Fr—uh, the Hardys and I have to see Mr. Hewitt."

The hurt showed in Ned's eyes. "Okay, then. See you later."

"Ned," Nancy called at his retreating back. But he didn't turn. He pretended that he didn't hear her call after him.

"Sorry about that," Frank murmured softly.

"Don't be. It wasn't your fault. You were only trying to help."

Irritation blended with remorse in Nancy's heart. It just wasn't fair! Why had Ned assumed the worst?

Chewing her thumbnail, Nancy realized what a mess she was in. Ned probably thinks I have something going with Frank, she thought. How do I convince him I don't?

The irony of it was that if it weren't for Ned

she would go for Frank Hardy. They had so much in common. She cast a surreptitious glance at Frank's profile. He was really cute!

Nancy tried to put the disloyal thought out of her mind. A tidal wave of guilt swept over her.

What's wrong with me? she asked herself. How could I even think such a thing? Ned's the one I love . . . the only guy for me.

Deep down, Nancy knew, that was true. But as she and Frank walked up to Joe, she couldn't help wondering what it would feel like to kiss Frank Hardy.

"Mr. Hewitt?" Nancy tapped on the frosted glass of his office door. Frank and Joe were standing next to her.

Joe peered through the frosted glass. "Anybody home?"

"The lights are on," Nancy said. "Maybe Hewitt stepped out." She tapped her foot impatiently.

Frank tried the knob, and the door swung wide. Frank peered inside. "Mr. Hewitt?"

Glen Hewitt lay behind his desk on his side with his mouth open, and the fingers of his outflung hands curled and limp. His face was as slack, pale, and lifeless as that of a corpse!

Chapter Fourteen

NANCY TORE ACROSS the room. Kneeling beside Hewitt, she picked up his hand and felt his wrist. Hewitt's pulse beat was fading fast.

"Frank! He's dying!"

"Joe, call an ambulance!" Frank put his ear to the man's chest as Joe picked up the phone. "His heart just stopped."

Frank knelt beside the stricken man and placed both hands just beneath Hewitt's ribcage. "Nancy, we need to try CPR. Open his mouth, pinch his nostrils shut, take deep breaths, and blow air into his lungs. Got it?"

Nodding, Nancy did as she was told. Meanwhile, Frank, keeping his arms straight, pushed down hard on the man's rib cage.

With each thrust, Frank counted, "*One* and two and three and four . . ."

An ambulance siren crescendoed in volume. Nancy kept giving Mr. Hewitt air. With her thumb she felt a faint but steady pulse in his throat.

Frank looked up at Joe. "I think his heart's beating again."

The three continued to keep Hewitt breathing, until the paramedics arrived. They wheeled in a portable oxygen unit and took over from Frank and Nancy. One slipped an oxygen mask over Hewitt's mouth. Then, as gently as possible, they lifted him onto a gurney.

"How is he?" Frank asked.

The crew chief sighed as they wheeled Hewitt out of the office. "Not good. He's in severe shock. The E.R. doctor's standing by at the hospital." Then he showed Frank and Nancy a grateful smile. "Good job on the CPR, people. You saved the man's life."

Two Santa Teresa police officers showed up as Hewitt was being pushed into the ambulance. Frank and Joe took them aside and explained what had happened.

Meanwhile, Nancy wandered back into Hewitt's office. Her practiced eye scanned the interior, seeking clues. An open book lay on the desk. She gave it a closer look.

The book was entitled *Sports Medicine—Theory and Practice.* One page displayed a color picture of a pole vaulter. The text on the opposite page gave a long description of drug use among athletes:

> Steroids, fat soluble or water based, can be administered either orally or by injection. . . .
>
> Steroids can have long-term serious side effects, including cancer of the liver and fits of irrational temper, a condition known as *roid rage.* . . .
>
> For these reasons, steroids are available only through a doctor's prescription. . . .
>
> One of the most commonly prescribed steroids is sold under the brand name Dynazol.

Why was Glen Hewitt reading up on steroids?

After the police left, Frank and Joe joined her. "Take a look at this," Frank said.

He handed her a charred slip of paper. Tilting it toward the light, Nancy could make out a series of printed numbers—a decimal code, only half of which was legible. The rest faded into scorched black carbon.

"I found it on the floor, near where we found Hewitt," Frank explained. "It's photocopy paper, the kind they use in library copiers. Hewitt must have copied an old newspaper article. Look at the date. Two years ago."

Joe scratched his head, puzzled. "I don't get it. Why would Hewitt go to the trouble of making a library copy and then burn it?"

"You're assuming that he's the one who burned it," Nancy replied. She grabbed a blank piece of paper from Hewitt's desk, wrapped up the burnt slip of paper, then put it in her back pocket. "If you don't mind, I'd like to check this out."

"No problem . . ." Voice fading, Joe stared suspiciously at Hewitt's coffee mug.

"What is it, Joe?" Nancy asked.

He pointed to the semicircle of white foam rimming the mug. "Maybe nothing, but when I offered to get Hewitt's coffee yesterday, he ordered it black. So why did he take it with cream today?"

"Good question." Grabbing a paper napkin, Frank dipped it into the mug and caught a dollop of foam. "I think we'd better get this analyzed."

A cool chill embraced them as they left the field house. The sun had slid behind a bank of dark clouds, and the wind had come up, carrying the smell of rain.

"Do you mind if we stop by the dorm to pick up my jacket?" Joe asked.

"Why not?" Frank answered. "It's on the way."

When they arrived at their room in Rondileau Hall, Frank spied a slip of white paper jutting out from under their door. He opened it, scowled, then showed it to Nancy and Joe.

> Found something interesting. May be important. Need to talk to you right away. See me when you get back.
>
> G. Hewitt

"He was on to something," Joe said grimly. "Somebody must have found out and put a little surprise in his coffee."

"Let's get to the lab," Frank replied. "I want to find out what that surprise was."

Two hours later Nancy and Joe watched in a chemistry lab while Frank finished mixing chemicals to do the final tests on the powder they'd found in Hewitt's mug. Nancy paced the floor impatiently. Joe sat on a lab stool, thumbing distractedly through a copy of *Science News.*

Restless, Nancy said, "I'm going to call the hospital to see how Hewitt's doing."

"Good idea, Nancy." Joe looked impatiently at his brother. "Come on, Frank. You don't have to try for the Nobel prize."

Nancy left the lab and stepped into a phone booth at the end of the hall. She called the hospital's emergency room and asked to speak to the physician in charge.

"Dr. Khatabi here," a voice answered in a minute.

"Doctor, my name is Nancy Drew. I work for Mr. Hewitt. I was wondering if he's all right."

"You're the girl who found him, yes?"

"That's right."

"Mr. Hewitt is in critical condition. We've moved him to intensive care."

"Do you have any idea what happened?" she asked.

"It appears that he had an extreme allergic reaction, resulting in sudden cardiac arrest."

Allergic reaction! Nancy's eyes widened. Her mind went back to a conversation with Hewitt when he explained he had an allergy to penicillin. She told the doctor what she knew.

He quietly gasped. "Thank you for telling me, Ms. Drew." Nancy heard him turn away from the phone to tell the nurse to prepare an injection. Then his voice grew louder again. "Ms. Drew, I have to go, but can you give me a number where I can reach you if there's any change in his condition?"

Nancy gave him her telephone number at Banning Hall and also Sigrid Larsen's.

After hanging up, she ran back into the lab. "I think we've IDed that foam. It's *penicillin!*"

"What?" Frank looked up from his test tubes.

"Frank, I just talked to the hospital," Nancy said. "They said Hewitt's had the kind of shock that comes from an allergic reaction."

"And he was allergic to penicillin," Joe added.

"Ridder has struck again," Nancy said simply.

Frank rested his hands on the lab counter. "You're saying Ridder found out about Mr. Hewitt's allergy, sneaked into his office, and poured penicillin in his coffee? This doesn't sound like his work."

Nancy nodded her head. "You're right, it doesn't. If it was Ridder, where's the telltale chess piece?"

"Exactly."

"But, no, it had to be Ridder," Nancy said after a minute. "Who else could it have been?"

"Maybe we're on the wrong track. Maybe that note Hewitt left for us has nothing to do with Ridder," suggested Joe. "Frank, you told me that Dave Gillespie threatened Mr. Hewitt, right?"

"Right. Nancy and I were there when Hewitt and Gillespie had it out," Frank said.

Nancy's throat tightened. Thinking of the charred slip, she wondered if Hewitt had dug up some new evidence in the Juan Valverde case.

She thought about Bess for a moment. Then she took one look at the Hardys and knew they were thinking the very same thing.

Was Dave Gillespie really a killer?

Chapter Fifteen

After a night filled with bad dreams, Nancy knew she had to tell Bess her suspicions about Dave Gillespie. Nancy pressed up close to the glass in the broadcasters' booth, peering down at the Parade of Athletes. The column proceeded slowly around the track. When each team marched by, the crowd's roar of welcome drifted up from the stands.

She tried to enjoy the spectacle, but her mind kept returning to the case and Ned. She had tried to call him last night, but he wasn't in before she went to bed. That day she'd called him three times, but he never could come to the phone.

"Nancy, take a look at this." Frank brought her back to the present—and the case.

Turning, she saw Frank standing in front of the battery of TV monitors. The center screen displayed a close-up of the U.S. team. Dave Gillespie's face appeared, looking taut and troubled.

"There's someone who doesn't look too happy," she murmured.

"Don't worry, Nancy." Frank gently draped his right arm over Nancy's shoulders. "Bess can take care of herself. Besides, there's no reason for Dave to go after Bess. And with Joe and George marching with the Norwegians, we're covered."

A TV technician walked up to them. "Excuse me, are you kids supposed to be here?"

"Games security." Frank flipped open his small leather ID folder. "We're looking for Mr. Crofton."

"Over there." The technician pointed out a tall, gangly man with a shock of dark brown hair.

Nancy and Frank went over and introduced themselves. George Crofton, Mr. Hewitt's replacement, looked pretty worried.

"A hundred thousand," he muttered, showing them a haggard look. "A hundred thousand spectators. It's a madhouse!"

"How's Mr. Hewitt doing?" Nancy asked.

"His condition's stabilized, but he's still in a coma," Crofton replied. "Look, I know why you're here, and I'm sorry, but I can't spare any of our people. I need them for crowd control. I'm afraid you kids are on your own."

Nancy tried to get a word in. "Couldn't you at least station someone—"

"I'm spread thin as it is. Mr. Overton won't let me hire any more off-duty cops." He moved away, his face apologetic. "Look, I've got to run. Let me know how you make out."

After he left, Frank turned to face Nancy, and backed against the glass booth. "I guess we really are on our own. And we're running out of time. Joe and I will question anyone who came and went from Hewitt's office yesterday."

"Okay." Nancy picked up her purse. "Good luck. I'll head for the library to check out that charred paper we found."

"Good idea."

Nancy started down the stairs, then turned back to Frank with a laugh. "Do you have any idea where the library is?" she asked.

Frank pointed west across the stadium, beyond Banning Hall and in the same direction as the ocean. "I think it's that way. But if you reach the sea, you've gone too far," he joked.

"Thanks, Frank."

With Frank's directions, Nancy found the

library fairly easily. Pushing open the glass doors, Nancy saw that the library was nearly deserted. A fortyish-looking woman stood sentry at the front desk. The brass nameplate on the counter read Mrs. Rowley.

Nancy introduced herself as a member of Games security and showed the librarian the scorched paper. Holding it gingerly, Mrs. Rowley peered at it over her glasses.

"You're right. This paper did come from our copier." She nodded in the direction of the microfilm readers in the middle of the nearby periodical room. "They stamp the copy with a serial number that corresponds to the article and newspaper."

Nancy pointed to the long string of numbers. "What newspaper is this from?"

"The Santa Teresa *Sun-Chronicle,* our local paper."

"I'd like to have a look at that tape." Nancy paused. "If it's not too much trouble."

"Of course," Mrs. Rowley said cheerfully. "You're in luck. I haven't filed it yet. A Mr. Hewitt was in here yesterday looking at it."

Excitement quickened Nancy's heartbeat. "Did he say why he wanted it?"

"No." The librarian looked thoughtful. "But I do remember he was quite eager to see it."

With Mrs. Rowley's help, Nancy got a microfilm reader in the nearby room set up. Mrs.

Rowley showed her how to make copies of anything that appeared onscreen.

"If you need any help," she said finally, "I'll be right over there at the main desk."

"Thanks very much," Nancy said as she spun the reel through the machine.

Nancy hit the fast-forward button. Pages of newsprint whirled past her eyes. She was hoping a familiar name or phrase would strike her before she got to the actual article Hewitt had copied.

Minutes later a news story jumped off the screen at Nancy.

Sports Star Collapses After Race

> Juan Valverde, wide receiver for the Santa Teresa Mustangs and track and field star, died Saturday afternoon while running a marathon.
>
> Valverde, 17, of 1279 Durango Avenue, was pronounced dead on arrival at Schallert Memorial Hospital. The cause of death was heart failure, according to medical examiner Dr. Clayton Matthews.
>
> David Gillespie, 17, of 4457 Balboa Drive, Valverde's competitor in the two-man race, told police that the youth had collapsed while they were crossing the ridge ten miles up Mount Sabado.

Gillespie ran to the nearest house to summon help. Valverde was flown into Santa Teresa by medical evacuation helicopter. Despite efforts to revive him, the youth died en route.

Valverde is survived by his mother, Esperanza Valverde; three brothers, Miguel, Ramon, and Alberto; and three sisters, Angelina, Raquel, and Dolores.

That fits with what Hewitt believed, Nancy thought, her eyes narrowing. She pressed the fast-forward button again. There was a follow-up story in the next day's edition that she skipped over. In it, Juan's sister told her side of the story, that Dave had killed Juan because Juan had been dating Dave's former girlfriend.

Reading on, Nancy came across a story dealing with Juan's funeral. A scuffle had erupted outside the church between Dave Gillespie and one of Juan's cousins. Nancy frowned. If Dave had killed him, then why had he gone to Juan's funeral?

Nancy was also intrigued by the catalog of sports accomplishments. A champion all-around athlete, Juan had been named one of the Southern California Football Conference's high school All-Stars.

How had he managed that with a heart condition? Nancy wondered.

As she reached the end of the article, a sentence leaped out at her.

> Standing behind the pallbearers at the grave site are Juan's mother, Mrs. Valverde, his sisters, brothers, and his girlfriend, the renowned swimmer Tracy Reynolds.

Blinking in surprise, Nancy sat back in her chair.

So Tracy Reynolds was Juan's girlfriend! Nancy turned her eyes back to the photo accompanying that news story. A series of familiar faces peered out at her.

Three of the pallbearers were strong guys she recognized instantly: Kurt Schweigert, Lino Passano, and Jeff Cannon!

Beside the floral wreaths stood two somber girls—Grete Nordstrom and Rosalia Vargas!

They were *all* in Santa Teresa two years ago, when Juan Valverde died. And they all knew Juan. How was this possible?

Nancy rechecked the ID number on her charred copy. Then she frowned. It didn't match the ID number on the funeral story.

Neither did the previous day's story. Then she checked the original Valverde obituary. Still no match!

Nancy frowned. If Hewitt hadn't copied the Valverde stories, then what had he copied?

It took the better part of an hour, but Nancy finally found a number that matched. She stared at the screen, puzzled.

State Police Probe Drug Use

The state attorney general's office today announced a crackdown on the use of steroids by high school athletes.

Recent reports of the use of the drug Dynazol by Southern California Football Conference teams prompted the investigation.

Last week Coach Andrew Stevens was inspecting lockers at El Dorado High School when he found bottles containing Dynazol capsules.

Steroids? Nancy squinted at the screen. Why would Hewitt bother to make a copy of that story?

In a flash Nancy remembered the open book on Hewitt's desk. He had been reading up on steroids, too.

But why? What did any of this have to do with Ridder?

After making a copy of the steroids article, Nancy rewound the tape, removed it from the spool, and carried it back to Mrs. Rowley's desk.

"Did you find what you were looking for?" Mrs. Rowley asked.

"I think so." Nancy handed her the tape. "But I'm very curious about something. A lot of athletes competing in the Games were in town two years ago."

"That's right." Mrs. Rowley rolled a pencil through her long fingers. "Santa Teresa hosted a small invitational competition then."

"Do any athletes come here regularly to train?"

"Quite a few. Kurt Schweigert. Lino Passano. Rosalia Vargas. Joe Kanaga—"

"You know them all by name?" Nancy was impressed.

"I'm a sports widow." Mrs. Rowley smiled archly. "That's all my husband talks about at the dinner table—which celebrity athlete is in town."

Thanking the librarian, Nancy walked out and headed back to her dorm.

So all of their main suspects had been at Juan's funeral, Nancy thought. But why? Obviously they were all acquainted, but that was all she could deduce.

And what was the connection, if any, to Ridder and Juan Valverde's death? Was Dave Gillespie the common denominator? Or another one of the athletes? Had competition driven one of them to murder?

Reaching Banning Hall, Nancy pulled open the door and stepped into the cool lobby. She quickly checked her mailbox—it was empty—and made her way to the stairs. At the last minute she decided to take the elevator.

Nancy was watching the lights on the elevator descend to the first floor, trying to make some sense of what she had learned.

She never heard the approaching footsteps. By the time she sensed that someone was standing behind her, it was too late.

A large hand clamped itself across her mouth. Then she felt a tight grip wrench her arm behind her back.

"Don't move!" A hoarse voice whispered in her ear. "Or else."

Chapter Sixteen

BEFORE SHE COULD REACT, Nancy's captor pushed her into the mailroom and slammed the door.

Lights blinked on overhead.

Turning around, Nancy was face-to-face with Dave Gillespie. Her mouth dropped open in shock.

Sweat gleamed on Dave's handsome face. "Look," he said. "You've got to hear me out."

Nancy eyed him warily. If Dave meant to hurt her, he would probably have done so by now. Still, she wasn't taking any chances.

"What were you doing at the library?" Dave asked.

"That's none of your business. What are *you* doing, dragging me in here?" Nancy countered.

"You're a detective, aren't you?"

Nancy feigned a look of disbelief. "I'm a nutrition major. You have a strange imagination, Gillespie."

"I've been talking to Bess. She told me all about the places you've been—New York, L.A., Hawaii. But whenever I asked what you were doing there, Bess somehow managed to change the subject." Dave stared at her. "You're an out-of-state PI, aren't you? Hewitt hired you to get the goods on me."

Nancy took a deep breath and tried to calm herself. "Let me ask you something, Dave. If you're as innocent as you claim to be, why are you spying on me?"

He looked a little embarrassed. "I don't have a choice. I *have* to find out what Hewitt has on me."

"Why don't you ask him?"

"Are you kidding? He's the one trying to get me sent up!" Despair twisted Dave's features. "Look, I *didn't* kill Juan!"

"His sister Angelina has a different story."

"Oh, that's great, Ms. Detective! I suppose you talked to her?"

Nancy decided to run a bluff. "That's right. And the staff at the hospital. You spent an awful lot of time in the records department, Dave."

"That was my job!"

"Is that where you found out about Juan's heart condition?"

"Everybody in school knew about that. Juan used to joke about it. 'Hold it, guys. Can I sneak past you? I've got a delicate heart.'" Dave sounded as if he was trying to convince himself. "Juan's heart gave out—that's all. It wasn't my fault!"

Nancy kept quiet. She let Dave go on, waiting to see what else he might say.

Dave shook his head helplessly. "You don't know what I went through two years ago. Angelina told everyone I killed her brother. Hewitt was building a case against me. Even my own parents had doubts."

"If you had nothing to do with Juan's death, then you have nothing to worry about," Nancy said softly.

"It doesn't matter! Hewitt decided I was guilty, and that was all that counted. I know how cops work. Maybe if Hewitt dies, they'll try to pin that on me, too!"

Nancy could understand why he was so worried. "You did look pretty guilty after that fight at the dance."

"I know, I know!" Dave buried his face in his hands. "I was just so angry. Tracy and

I—well, I thought she was *my* girl. And there she was at the dance with Juan. I'll be honest, I wanted to hurt him, but not kill him. You've got to believe me."

Then something clicked. Nancy remembered the article Hewitt had copied about the steroids scandal at El Dorado High School at the same time Dave, Juan, and Tracy were at Santa Teresa High.

"Dave, have you ever heard the expression *roid rage?*" Nancy asked, waiting to see his reaction.

Dave looked up suddenly. "Sure. Athletes who use steroids start blowing their tempers at the least little—" Understanding filled his face. "Hold on! If you're saying I was— Forget it, lady! Our school was clean. I was mad at Juan, sure, but steroids had nothing to do with it. Nobody in our school was on the stuff."

She looked at him carefully. Was Dave Gillespie telling the truth? she wondered.

If he had been been taking steroids, and Juan found out about it, then Dave might have killed him to protect his secret.

Nancy decided to take the offensive. "Why did you challenge Juan to a marathon if you knew he had a heart condition?"

Nancy watched as Dave's angry defiance ebbed and was replaced by what seemed like a blend of guilt and remorse. He sat down at the table that was used to sort mail.

"I couldn't take it, Nancy," he said, resting his elbows on the table. "I couldn't stand losing Tracy to him. Juan was always bragging, 'I'm number one.' I wanted to show him up, that's all. I figured that if I won, people would know who was top jock at Santa Teresa High. And I thought—maybe—I might get Tracy back. I never dreamed . . ." His voice choked. "How was I supposed to *know?* Juan had been a runner since junior high. His heart condition was minor and never stopped him from doing anything."

Dave brushed awkwardly at his eyes. "I even thought he was horsing around when I first saw him lying in the road. But when I rolled him over, he was red faced and gasping. I ran for help. Doc Matthews was waiting for us at the hospital. They wheeled Juan right into intensive care. But it was too late. He—" Dave squeezed his eyes shut, unable to go on. "When it was all over, Doc Matthews told me that Juan had ruptured his aorta."

"Take it easy, Dave," Nancy said. The boy was really upset as he relived his rival's death. Dave sighed, and with his strong fingers wiped the tears from his cheek. "If I'd known what was going to happen, I *never*— I didn't mean for it to happen, Nancy. I'm not a murderer! *I'm not!*"

Nancy realized what an incredible burden of guilt Dave Gillespie had been carrying around for the past two years. He blamed himself for Juan Valverde's death. That was why he had gone to the boy's funeral. Deep down, Dave must have felt that if he had never made that challenge, Juan might still be alive.

Nancy felt convinced of his innocence now. She sat down, too, and reached for Dave's hands. "Dave, you mustn't blame yourself. That won't bring Juan back. It'll only ruin your life."

"I can't help feeling responsible."

"You may have been a little foolish. But Juan accepted the challenge—he decided to take part in the race. I don't think anyone could say you're a murderer."

Patting his shoulder, Nancy stood up. "Try not to let it haunt you. Think about your future."

"Thank you for believing me, Nancy," Dave said.

Nancy let herself out of the mailroom, leaving Dave alone to cope with his grief.

After lunch Nancy sat on a sideline bench with Frank and Joe. In front of them, the athletes were warming up. A capacity crowd filled the stands. Farther out on the field, George Crofton chatted with a security guard. Jim Overton, in the official navy blazer and white pants, sauntered along the cinder track, waving and shaking hands with everyone.

"Did you make any progress this morning?" Nancy asked.

"Not much," Frank admitted. "How did you do?"

Nancy quickly described her trip to the library and her conversation with Dave Gillespie.

"I still don't understand where the steroids come into it," Frank remarked when she was finished. "You said Dave swore that no one at his school was taking them."

"Gillespie may be lying," Joe commented.

"That's true," Nancy admitted. "But I don't think he knew about it. I think Dave is innocent."

"If that's the case, then the steroid connection goes nowhere," Joe said.

"Not necessarily," Frank pointed out. "Maybe someone was supplying steroids to some team members that Dave didn't know about. Juan might have found out and threatened to turn him or her in."

"But how would that have killed him? He died from the run. Wait a minute. Maybe Juan himself was on steroids," suggested Nancy.

"We can check that theory awfully fast," said Joe. "We can talk to Dr. Matthews. He signed Juan's death certificate."

"I say we find out if any of our suspects are on steroids," Frank suggested. He stood up. "Maybe Juan's death and Ridder are connected by steroids. How, we don't know yet. But if we keep digging . . ."

"And athletes generally know who's beefing up their performance with steroids. If we ask around, I'm sure we can find out who's used them," Joe said.

"Good hunting." Nancy replied.

Nancy picked her way through the crowded bleachers, looking for George and Sigrid, who were watching the day's events. A forest of national flags rippled in the stands surrounding her. Huge hand-lettered signs rose for the benefit of TV cameras. *"La Belle France Toujours"* and *"Victoria Para España"* competed with *"We're From Billings!"* and *"Hi, Mom!"*

She caught a glimpse of George and Sigrid in front of two burly Austrians. She skirted the Austrians, hopped over someone's portable ice chest, and gratefully dropped into the empty seat beside George and Sigrid.

"Good timing, Nan. You're just in time for the men's one-hundred-ten-meter hurdles," George said.

Nancy scanned the field and the other events already in progress. "I thought the hurdles took place on the second day."

"Good memory, Nan," George said. "Usually it does, but earlier the Games committee made an announcement that they're switching the events. They're holding the hundred-meter dash tomorrow instead."

"Isn't that a little strange?" Nancy asked.

"I guess. But they didn't explain why they had to do it." George's attention was already on the field.

Nancy noticed the bandage on Ragnar's leg. Nudging George, she asked, "Isn't that cut going to hold Ragnar back in this event?"

"Oh, no. It's only a surface cut. Dr. Matthews okayed him this morning." Cupping her hands to her mouth, George hollered, "Go for the gold, Ragnar!"

One by one the athletes crouched at their starting blocks. Nancy watched as Ragnar placed the cleated soles of his shoes against the blocks, raised himself up into a crouch, placed his fingertips on the cinder track, and stared straight ahead.

The referee lifted his pistol. "On your marks . . ."

As one, the competitors stiffened.

"Get set!"

Bang! The athletes took off with the gunshot. Dave Gillespie immediately grabbed the lead. Then Ragnar broke away from the pack, catching up with him on the first turn.

George and Sigrid leapt from their seats, shouting encouragement. Most of the crowd was now watching the hurdlers.

Breathing in measured gasps, Ragnar approached the first row of hurdles at top speed. He left the ground, right leg extended, soaring with clockwork precision and grace. After clearing the first hurdle, he quickened his stride. Dave Gillespie was right on his heels.

Dave and Ragnar took the second row of hurdles dead even. Ragnar landed on the ball of his right foot, dug his toes into the cinders, and hurled himself onward.

Ragnar cleared the third set a second ahead of Dave. Sweat poured down his face. His legs churned like pistons.

From where Nancy stood, it seemed to her that the hurdle Ragnar was heading for was slightly out of line with those next to it.

With a grunt of effort, Ragnar left the ground in a classic leap. Despite his concentration, his legs drooped just a little. Nancy watched as Ragnar's left knee banged the edge of the hurdle.

Then something went wrong. Instead of falling forward, the hurdle stood like a brick wall. The crowd looked on in horror as Ragnar clutched his left leg, screamed, and tumbled headfirst onto the track!

Chapter Seventeen

RAGNAR!" George and Sigrid screamed in unison.

Nancy jumped from her seat and raced down the stairs. The other runners stumbled over Ragnar as he rolled. Ragnar pulled himself into a sitting position on the track, his face a mask of agony. A pair of Games medics hurried down the track with a stretcher.

Moments later Nancy, George, and Sigrid met the stretcher at the gate. Sigrid clutched her brother's hand. "Ragnar, are you all right?"

He nodded vigorously. "I think it's nothing," he said. Features tensing, he straightened his leg. "For some reason the hurdle didn't fall over as it was supposed to."

Nancy watched as Overton and the stripe-shirted referee hurried toward them. When the referee found out what had happened, he lifted his whistle. "I'm going to void this race." He blew a shrill blast and signaled to the Games committee booth. The stadium began to murmur.

Soon, a voice came over the loudspeaker. "The hundred-and-ten-meter hurdles will be rescheduled for tomorrow," it announced.

Nancy followed the referee down the track to inspect Ragnar's hurdle. He gave the hurdle a solid thump with his fist. It quivered but didn't fall.

Kneeling, Nancy closed one eye and looked along the top. Her lips tightened. The hurdle was an inch taller than the ones next to it.

Then Nancy noticed the dull gray metal filling the open cylinders at the base of the hurdle's legs. A touch told her what they were.

"Lead plugs," Nancy murmured. "They made the hurdle too heavy to fall over."

The referee saw what Nancy was pointing to and made a sound of disgust. "I'd better report this to Mr. Overton."

As the referee walked away, Nancy probed the cinders with her fingertips. She wasn't at all surprised when she found a chess piece—the black knight!

Overton and a small contingent of Games dignitaries came walking up to her. "What are you doing, Ms. Drew?"

Nancy showed him the chess piece. "It was Ridder again. He rigged the hurdle to spill Ragnar."

"How?" Overton's question was a shout of frustration.

Nancy quickly explained the situation.

Clenching his fists, Overton snapped, "What am I supposed to do now?" He fired a quick glance at the crowd of reporters waiting at the gate. "When they find out about Ridder, we're sunk!" He sighed heavily. "Look, I hate to say this, but maybe those Larsen kids should withdraw."

"Mr. Overton, that's not fair," Nancy said emphatically as they headed for the gate. "Ragnar and Sigrid trained to compete. More than anyone else, you should understand what this means to them."

"I know what it means." He deliberately avoided Nancy's look. "And I sympathize with both of them. But I have the Games to think about. If Ridder keeps sabotaging the events, we'll be ruined. Maybe if the Larsens went back to Norway, this harassment would stop."

"You don't know that," Nancy added quickly.

Stopping short, Overton turned to face her. "No, I don't. But I do know this, Ms. Drew.

You and the Hardys have had no luck in catching this nut." His mouth tightened grimly before he went on. "And I have to do whatever I can to save the Games. I'm going to ask the committee to make a decision about whether or not to ask the Larsens to withdraw."

When they reached the gate, the TV field crews descended on Overton. Nancy avoided the crowd of TV cameras, slipping into the gateside crowd.

As she climbed the stadium stairs, Nancy studied the chess piece in the palm of her hand.

There were things about Ridder that made no sense at all. Why did he keep switching back and forth between pranks and murder attempts? Did Ridder really want to kill Ragnar or not?

Frowning, Nancy pocketed the chess piece. The only real evidence that Ridder wanted to kill Ragnar was when he threw that javelin.

Nancy considered her suspects. Lino, Kurt, and Jeffrey were all expert javelin throwers. Grete Nordstrom, too. Dave Gillespie was a sloppy thrower. But what if that was only an act? What if Dave had hurled the javelin at Bess, hoping to convince people how clumsy he was?

Nancy found the Larsens at the athletes' refreshment table. Ragnar was sipping from a tall protein shake. Sigrid fussed over her brother. George stood off to one side, talking to the Hardys. Other athletes had gathered around to commiserate with Ragnar.

Jeff Cannon slapped the table. "What's wrong with that maintenance crew? Didn't they bother to measure those hurdles?"

"Take it easy," Kurt said soothingly. "We'll do the hurdles tomorrow."

"I was all set to do it today!" Jeff complained, pacing about nervously. He kept wiping his mouth with the back of his hand.

Frank Hardy came over to Nancy. "What happened out there, Nancy?" Frank asked.

She quickly explained. "And he left this," Nancy concluded, showing Frank the chess piece.

Joining Frank and Nancy, Joe whispered, "What's next?"

"There's nothing more we can do here. Let's have that talk with Dr. Matthews," Nancy suggested. "I keep wondering about that clipping Hewitt made."

Joe gave her a thoughtful look. "What about it?"

"Remember the first time we talked to Mr. Hewitt, Joe?" Frank asked. When his brother nodded, Frank went on. "He mentioned that 'something funny' was going on in Santa Teresa at the time Juan Valverde was killed. Then he cut out that article on the steroids scandal in El Dorado. I think the two have to be related."

"But when we asked the other athletes, they claimed Gillespie was never mixed up with steroids," Joe reminded him.

"But maybe one of our other suspects could have been," Frank said. "Remember, they were all in Santa Teresa at the time of Juan's death. How well did they know Juan? Somehow this all has to be connected. Dr. Matthews might be able to tell us."

"We have too many suspects and too many varying motives. We have to narrow it down somehow," Nancy replied.

Frank nodded. "She's right, Joe. We've got Ridder, his booby traps, the Juan Valverde case, and that old steroids scandal. I think Mr. Hewitt's the key. He found out something, and it made our culprit nervous. We can't afford to ignore any lead."

Nancy and the Hardys agreed to meet in the parking lot in a few minutes. While Nancy went off to the dorm to change, Frank and Joe checked on the Larsens.

"How are you doing, Ragnar?" Joe asked.

"A little better." Pursing his lips Ragnar rose stiffly. "But if I'm going to run this afternoon," he added with a groan, "I'd better hit the whirlpool."

Frank braced him. "We'll walk you there," he said.

In the men's training room a weary Ragnar Larsen slid into the bubbling whirlpool. Frank stepped away from the porcelain rim, feeling the steam moisten his face.

"Are you going to be okay?" Joe asked.

Ragnar nodded. "I'll be fine. I'll soak for an hour, then do a few squats. Let me know how you make out with Dr. Matthews."

"We will," Frank promised. "It's funny no one else is around," Frank mumbled to his brother.

"They're all out on the track. All set to meet Nancy?" Joe asked. He noticed the pensive expression on his older brother's face. "Uh-oh! I hear the big wheels turning. What's on your mind, Frank?"

"I'm still confused about Ridder's motive," Frank said, stroking his chin. "Why did he bother to send all those warning messages to Sigrid if his purpose was to eliminate Ragnar?"

"Maybe he thought Sigrid could talk Ragnar into going home."

"But that isn't what happened, Joe. If anything, those warnings convinced Ragnar to stay in the Games."

"What are you getting at, brother?"

"I'm wondering if Ragnar really is our pal's target. Joe, what if the purpose of these attacks is to frighten *Sigrid* out of the games?"

Comprehension lit up Joe's face. "If Sigrid drops out, the other girls all stand a better chance of winning."

Suddenly a low moan drifted out from the whirlpool room.

Frank lifted his chin. "Ragnar?"

There was no reply.

"Ragnar!" Frank shouted.

In response, they heard an incoherent mumble in Norwegian.

Exchanging a sharp look with Joe, Frank rushed forward and pushed into the room. They saw Ragnar leaning against the porcelain rim, his eyes closed, his head rolling from side to side.

Then, slowly, Ragnar slipped farther down into the whirlpool. His blond head disappeared beneath the steaming water!

Chapter Eighteen

"GRAB HIM! HE'LL DROWN!" Joe shouted.

The Hardys jumped into the whirlpool. Ragnar had disappeared under the steam and bubbles. Frank waved his arms beneath the churning surface. Hot, moist air billowed into his face.

"Frank! Here!"

Joe hauled Ragnar above the water. The boy mumbled incoherently, occasionally spitting up water. Frank helped his brother carry him out of the pool.

After putting Ragnar on the bench, Frank opened his mouth and tried to breathe some air into his lungs. Moments later, Ragnar rolled over and choked on what water was still in his lungs. Frank helped him lie back on the bench. Ragnar murmured in slurred Norwegian.

Frank lifted the athlete's eyelid. His pupil failed to respond to the light.

"He's been drugged," Frank said, remembering the protein shake Ragnar had been drinking earlier.

"Somebody wanted Ragnar to pass out in the whirlpool," Joe said solemnly.

"You read my mind," Frank said. He looked at Ragnar, who seemed to be coming around slowly. "Come on, get an ambulance to the clinic and then find Nancy. This'll give us a chance to talk to Dr. Matthews, too."

The campus clinic was in the Krieger Building, a half mile from the stadium. Sun flashes glimmered on the wide windows of the modern sand-colored building.

Nancy and the Hardys followed the gurney carrying Ragnar through the sliding glass door into the pastel-walled reception area.

The nurse stepped into action. "I'll call the doctor," she said, picking up the phone.

Surprise blossomed on Dr. Matthews's face as he emerged from his inner office and saw Ragnar. "What happened?"

Frank explained, and the doctor took charge

of Ragnar. "Run a complete series of blood tests," he ordered.

"Do you have a minute to talk, Doctor?" Frank asked, after Ragnar's blood had been drawn. "We have a few questions to ask you."

"Certainly. Is this about Sigrid Larsen?" Dr. Matthews asked once they were seated in his office. "If you ask me, that girl shouldn't be competing. The last time I saw her, she was an emotional wreck."

"She's better now," Nancy answered. "Actually, Doctor, we're interested in an old patient of yours."

"Juan Valverde," Frank said grimly.

Dr. Matthews dropped the stethoscope he had been handling on his desk. He said, "Juan passed away two years ago."

Frank's tone was professional. "Exactly what did he die of, Doctor?"

"Clinically speaking, the term is *aortic stenosis,"* the doctor replied. "Juan was born with a defective aorta. That's the main artery in the heart. The walls of Juan's aorta were slightly thinner than a normal person's. The condition is uncommon but rarely fatal. In Juan's case, the strain of running that marathon, particularly at high altitude, raised his blood pressure and triggered the rupture, killing him."

"Was Juan aware of all that?" Nancy asked.

The doctor nodded. "When he was six years

old, the school nurse noticed his irregular heartbeat and referred him to me. I diagnosed his condition, prescribed treatment, and became his personal physician."

"And you let him compete," Joe observed.

"I advised against it, but Juan wouldn't listen. Since I couldn't talk him out of it, I gave him an exercise regime to follow, one that would strengthen his cardiovascular system. Frankly, I'm surprised Juan ever made the team. He was such a frail boy—even for a runner. But he really filled out during his sophomore year."

Suddenly Nancy was back in Hewitt's office, staring down at that open book on his desk.

The first reported use of steroids was in the early 1950s. Soviet athletes reportedly used them to build up bulk and mass in their bodies.

Then she remembered the news clipping Hewitt had taken from the library—that story about steroid use at nearby El Dorado High School.

"Did you know much about the high school players, Doctor?" Nancy asked.

He shrugged. "A bit. I gave some of those boys their physicals."

Conscious of Frank's curious glance, Nancy went on. "Did they hang around much with the other conference teams? Like El Dorado?"

Suspicion tightened the doctor's face. "What are you getting at?"

"Doc, Juan must have really filled out to make it as a football player in addition to his abilities as a runner," said Joe, folding his arms casually. "When exactly did he 'fill out'?"

"The summer after his sophomore year," Dr. Matthews said tersely.

"In other words, Juan left school in June looking like a skinny tenth grader," Joe added. "And then he came back in the fall ready to make the football team. Don't you think that's just a little strange?"

"I'm afraid I don't see the point, young man."

"Let's look at the timetable, Doctor," said Frank crisply. "Juan fills out the summer before his junior year. He makes the varsity squad that fall. A big steroids scandal breaks over in El Dorado. Then the Santa Teresa police hear rumors of steroid use at their school."

"I never heard of—" the doctor began.

"But Hewitt did," Frank interrupted. "At first he thought Dave Gillespie was the one mixed up with steroids, but the more he found out about Dave, the more he realized how wrong he was. Then Hewitt came up with a new bit of information—something that sent him running to the library two years later to check out the El Dorado steroids scandal. Somebody may have gotten nervous about that and poisoned him. I think Hewitt found out that *Juan Valverde* was on steroids."

"Impossible!" Dr. Matthews snapped.

"Not really," Nancy added evenly. "A lot of the same people who were in Santa Teresa at the time of Juan's death are back in town for these Games. And we've heard rumors of steroid use here at the Games."

"That whole thing is a tempest in a teapot," he replied. "There is no basis whatsoever to that rumor. I personally examined each of the competing athletes myself. No one is on steroids at these Games."

"Doctor, Dave Gillespie was the jock king at Santa Teresa High," Frank said. "Let's suppose for a moment that Juan took steroids hoping to match Dave's endurance in that race. Could those steroids have induced his fatal heart attack?"

Dr. Matthews wiped his lips. "They *might* have . . . *if* Juan had taken them. Steroids spur muscles into performing beyond their limits. And the heart is a muscle, you know. But there was no trace of steroids in Juan's bloodstream during the autopsy. I can personally attest to that."

The lab technician opened the door and gently interrupted their conversation. "Excuse me, Dr. Matthews," she said. "We've run the tests on Larsen, and he's ready to be examined."

Matthews waved the nurse off. "I'll be right out. Please excuse me," he addressed the three in his office.

After the doctor had gone, Joe whispered, "So no one's using steroids at the Games, eh? That's not what Kurt Schweigert told us."

"What are you talking about?" Nancy asked.

"When we talked to Schweigert, he said that he suspects certain athletes of using steroids, including Jeff Cannon."

Nancy let out a low whistle. Before the news could sink in, Frank turned to his brother.

"Joe, you did it again," he said.

"Did what, Frank?"

"Put things into perspective for me." Frank kept his voice at a whisper. "Matthews did the physicals on the competitors, right? If Kurt is right, and I think he is, then Matthews would have to know that Jeff Cannon is on steroids. That means Matthews is lying."

"It's even worse than that, Frank," Nancy said.

"What do you mean?"

"Matthews did the autopsy on Juan Valverde."

Joe's eyes widened. "Ohhhhh brother!"

"It's beginning to fit," muttered Frank, his expression grim. "Faced with Dave's challenge, Juan took a large dose just before the marathon. Matthews must have known that

Juan was on steroids. That's why he volunteered to do the autopsy. It put him in the perfect position to cover up. Any other doctor would have found it in Juan's bloodstream."

Nancy bit her lower lip and thought. "Frank, I'd bet it was Dr. Matthews who *gave* Juan the steroids," she said finally. "According to Hewitt's book, you can't get steroids legally without a prescription."

At once, the three of them glanced at the doctor's wall-mounted medicine chest.

Frank got out of his chair and stood beside the door. Then he nodded. "Nancy—Joe—give it a quick look. I'll stand guard."

Joe pulled the cabinet door open and fumbled through the medicine. "Your theory makes sense, Nancy. The suspects were all here two years ago. If one of them is on steroids, chances are Dr. Matthews is doing the supplying."

"Just as he did for Juan." Nancy stared at the dozens of little bottles on the shelves. She and Joe shifted them around, reading an unfamiliar medical name on each label.

Then a small amber bottle caught Nancy's eye.

"That's it!" she shouted, reading the label and remembering the open book on Hewitt's desk yet again. *"Dynazol!"*

Chapter Nineteen

THEY HEARD the sound of footsteps outside the door.

"Hurry!" Joe shouted. He swiftly put the bottles back in their proper places. Then Nancy eased the door shut. Together they made a cat-footed dash to the other side of the office and stood looking out the picture windows.

Frank opened the door suddenly. Dr. Matthews flinched in surprise, his hand reaching for the doorknob.

"There you are," said Frank, flashing a pleasant smile. "I was just about to come looking for you, Doctor. How's Ragnar doing?"

"I'm sending him back to the stadium. He'll be fine now. You were right, though. He'd been drugged with a light dose of tranquilizers." Nancy saw the doctor's gaze travel from Frank to her and Joe.

"I'm glad he's okay," Nancy said.

"We'll see ourselves out. Thanks." Frank held the door open for Nancy and Joe.

They left the building and found a quiet spot to talk. Leaning against a redbrick wall, Joe remarked, "So Matthews keeps Dynazol in his office. Pretty handy, eh?"

"We can assume he was supplying Juan Valverde," Frank added. "Chances are he's supplying people in the Games, too."

"So where do we go from here?" Nancy asked.

"I think Joe and I should check out the steroid connection," Frank said. "We need proof that Cannon—and anyone else, Lino for example—has been taking them before we can say for a fact that Matthews is supplying athletes now."

"That still leaves the Ridder trail cold, though," Nancy said.

"You're right," Joe said, shaking his head. "We don't know why Ridder is after the Larsens, except to get them out of the games."

"It could still be Dave. That may be what Hewitt was on his way to proving by going back over the Valverde case. But I was sure he was innocent." The three were quiet for a minute.

"Wait a minute!" Nancy banged her forehead with the palm of her hand. "We're missing the really important connection. We tied the Valverde case to Ridder because of Dave Gillespie. But it could be another person—not Dave—who is the connection."

"Like who?" Frank asked.

Nancy reminded Frank and Joe of what she had learned at the library. She glanced in the direction of Banning Hall. "I think I'm going to have a talk with Tracy Reynolds—if she's not competing now."

"You're right, Nancy! Tracy could be the missing connection. Good luck."

"Be careful," Nancy warned. "If Cannon is on steroids, he could be dangerous."

As they entered the locker room, Frank and Joe saw the decathlon athletes nervously milling around, awaiting the announcement of the shot put. Lino had a towel draped casually around his neck and was chatting with Kurt. Jeff Cannon sat on the bench in front of his locker, stretching and flexing his well-muscled arms. At his side rested a small, dark green gym bag.

Joe whispered, "I'll get him outside for a minute."

"Ten seconds is all I need, Joe."

"Help me out." Joe snapped his fingers, grimacing in frustration. "Give me the name of a popular British newspaper."

"The London *Daily Mail.*"

Standing beside the water fountain, Frank watched his brother hurry across the room.

"Hey, Jeff, some guy was looking for you a few minutes ago," said Joe, hooking his thumb over his shoulder. "What's-his-name of the London *Daily Mail.*"

Jeff stood up. His face turned eager. "Michael Ames?"

"Yeah, that's him. Something about an interview."

As Joe shepherded the British athlete out the door, the locker room's public-address speaker announced, "And now the third event of the decathlon—the shot put!"

The athletes filed out. Frank stole over to Jeff Cannon's locker. Opening the steel door, he scanned the top shelf. Nothing. Then Frank searched the pockets of Jeff's street clothes. No pills or capsules.

Then he saw Jeff's gym bag, sitting on the bench.

Frank unzipped it. His hand worked its way past cotton tank tops and towels. Suddenly he felt a strange bulge in one of the socks. Pulling it out, he folded back the fabric to expose a small plastic vial.

Too late, Frank heard the gym door's hinges squeak open.

"Here!" Jeff's furious voice rang out. "What do you think you're doing?"

Frank showed him the vial. "Is this what you came back for?"

Murderous rage distorted Jeff's face.

"How long have you been on Dynazol, Cannon?"

Instead of answering, Jeff Cannon threw himself at Frank. His muscled leg flew upward in a vicious kick. Frank ducked to the right. The cleats of Jeff's track shoes just missed Frank's chin.

Frank let him close in, waiting until Jeff's big hands settled on his shoulders. Then he cut loose with a karate combination—side chop to the ribs, fist to the stomach, elbow to the throat.

Jeff went down roaring. Frank rolled him onto his face, straddled him, and pinned both wrists. "Take it easy, Cannon."

Joe rushed in. "Are you okay, Frank?"

"Never better." Frank kept a firm grip on his captive. "Want to tell us about the Dynazol, Jeff?"

Jeff squirmed under Frank's grip, kicking and thrashing. "It's not mine! Not mine! Somebody planted it there."

"I guess that gym bag was the only safe place

for it," Joe remarked, helping Frank lift the boy to his feet. "Jocks carry their gym bags everywhere they go. Nobody thinks twice about it."

"Where did you get the steroids, Cannon?" asked Frank sternly.

"There's no law against it." Jeff's shoulders slumped in defeat.

"But it is against the Games' rules."

"I've got a legitimate prescription."

"From Dr. Matthews?" Frank asked.

Jeff's shocked glance took in both Hardys. "You know?"

Joe nodded grimly. "And now we want to hear all about it."

Sobbing in despair, Jeff began to talk.

Nancy strode briskly down the Banning Hall corridor, her mind clicking away. It was strange how the Ridder mystery kept blending with the old Valverde case. Of the three people involved in the romantic triangle at Santa Teresa High, two had reason to harm the Larsens. Dave Gillespie was one. And Tracy Reynolds was the other!

Her knuckles rapped on Tracy's door. Soft footfalls sounded on the carpet. The door swung open, revealing a smiling Tracy, her hair piled high on her head, wearing a shimmery blue unitard.

"Well! If it isn't our wandering nutritionist."

Tracy adjusted a disc-shaped practice weight on her wrist. "Come on in. I was just finishing an aerobic workout."

"Thank you." Nancy closed the door behind her.

"Your friend George is very good. I keep telling her she ought to try out for the U.S. team, but no soap." Her smile turned quizzical. "But you're not here to talk about George, are you?"

"Not exactly."

Tracy's smile turned crooked. Nancy went on. "I have a few questions to ask you about your old boyfriend—Juan Valverde."

Tracy drew her shoulders back, casting Nancy a wary look. "What about Juan?"

"I'll be honest with you, Tracy. Glen Hewitt thought Juan was murdered. He did some poking around. Then someone poisoned him."

"What's all this got to do with me?" Tracy challenged.

"Everybody at Santa Teresa High knew about Juan's heart condition—"

"It wasn't exactly a deep, dark secret," Tracy interrupted.

"But how many people knew he was taking steroids?" Nancy replied. "His doctor, certainly. Matthews was supplying him. Dave Gillespie, maybe. And then there's his girlfriend—"

Tracy's face flooded with indignation. "How *dare* you imply that I—"

"Whoever poisoned Mr. Hewitt had to know about Juan's steroids. You and Dave are the only two people from Santa Teresa High here at the Games."

"Look, there are plenty of people here who knew Juan. Why don't you go talk to *them,* huh?"

"But no one was as close to Juan as you. You had to know about the steroids. You and Dave. There are only two possibilities, Tracy. Either Juan gave himself the Dynazol boost he needed to win that marathon. Or else you or Dave poisoned him. And then poisoned Mr. Hewitt when he began to poke around in the Valverde case again."

"That's absurd!" Tracy snapped.

"Is it? Dave was pretty upset when Juan stole you away from him."

"Is *that* what Dave said?" Tracy lifted her gaze in exasperation. "Boys are so . . . nobody *stole* me, Nancy. I broke up with Dave of my own free will. Dave thought he was going to be a high school jock all his life. I wanted somebody more mature."

"Somebody like Juan?"

"That's right. Juan wanted to make his sports career pay off, trying to keep his name before the public. It was working, too. Juan already had a big offer to promote sportswear—"

Tracy stopped suddenly. Nancy caught a flicker of alarm in the girl's eyes. She was hiding something. But what?

Avoiding Nancy's look, Tracy went on. "I can't believe what you're telling me. Dave's not responsible for Juan's death. It was a stupid challenge. Juan never should have accepted it."

Nancy tried to keep the girl talking. "Someone's been trying to hurt Ragnar Larsen. Ragnar is Dave's main rival for the decathlon, the same way Juan was his rival two years ago. This could be the second time around for Dave."

"No!" Tracy screamed. "Dave's not like that! He'd never hurt anyone."

"All right, then let's suppose that Ragnar isn't the target. Let's say *Sigrid* is."

Tracy stared at her in confusion.

"Maybe the Valverde case has nothing to do with the Larsens, except as a smoke screen," Nancy continued. "Let's suppose that the culprit is one of Sigrid's rivals. Who's the only girl who knows enough about the Valverde case to successfully frame Dave Gillespie?"

"I don't *be-leeeeev—"* Tracy slapped the top of the chest of drawers. "For your information, Nancy Drew, I don't have to rig anything! I can beat Sigrid Larsen fair and square! I'm a professional! I don't have to stoop to dirty tricks to win a competition. Now, if you're finished—" Crossing the room in three angry strides, Tracy pulled open the door. "Get out!"

As Nancy turned to leave, her gaze zeroed in on the shelf above Tracy's chest of drawers. A plastic vial sat there. The pharmacy label read "Ampicillin—50 capsules."

Nancy frowned. Tracy seemed like the picture of good health. What was she doing with that prescription? Nancy was about to ask her when Tracy pushed her out of her room and slammed the door in her face.

That girl's hiding something, Nancy thought as she walked down the corridor. Then she heard the sound of running feet, punctuated by Frank's excited shout. "Nancy! Wait up!"

She halted at the elevator. "How did you guys make out?"

"We caught Cannon with a vial of Dynazol. He confessed everything. He was clued in to Matthews when he was here two years ago," Frank explained.

"Why did they all go to Juan's funeral—did he answer that?" Nancy asked.

"It was courtesy. They'd met Juan and he was an up-and-coming athlete—they went to honor him," Frank explained.

"There's more," Joe said. "Cannon says he saw Matthews on campus the night before your accident on the bleachers. Even worse, when I called the medical center to find out where Matthews was when we had our accident in the mountains, they said he was playing golf."

"I called the country club," Frank added. "Nobody at the pro shop remembers seeing him that morning."

"He's our boy." Joe aimed his thumb at the elevator. "Before he can skip, let's pick him up."

Nancy and the Hardys jogged across campus to the infirmary. The nurse's desk was vacant. Peering around the door jamb, Nancy spied Dr. Matthews hastily packing a nylon flight bag.

Frank entered first. "Got a minute, Doc?"

The physician looked up irritably. "What is it? I'm a busy man."

Joe came in second, gesturing at the flight bag. "I thought doctors didn't make house calls anymore."

Straightening up, Dr. Matthews took a backward step and rested his right arm on an instrument tray. "What do you people want?"

"We need your help on a case, Doctor," Frank said grimly.

Joe grinned. "We're calling it *The Case of the Missing Canteen.*"

Nancy came in right on cue. "But it was never missing, was it, Dr. Matthews? When the paramedics picked up Juan Valverde, they tossed his canteen into the helicopter. You found it when the chopper arrived at the hospital and destroyed it before they wheeled Juan into intensive care."

Beads of sweat sprouted above the doctor's eyebrows. "Why would I do *that?*" His fingers moved to cover one of the instruments.

Frank stepped forward. "Because you knew the canteen contained a dose of the Dynazol you'd given to Juan. You knew the police would test the water. You could fake the autopsy, but you couldn't influence the outcome of the police test. So you hid the canteen in the operating room and got rid of it later."

Dr. Matthews went white. In a flash, he snatched a razor-sharp scalpel from the tray. With one swift move, he swung the scalpel right at Nancy's face!

Chapter Twenty

NANCY HAD CAUGHT only a glimpse of the glittering blade rushing at her before Frank grabbed her around the waist. With a yank, he pulled her out of the way. The blade's tip zipped past her nose.

Dr. Matthews next swung at Joe, who did a quick sidestep, lifting his arms. The scalpel came close enough to nip a piece of fabric from his jacket. Joe used his left arm to block the doctor's next swing. Then, planting his feet, he let loose with a haymaker that caught Matthews in the chin.

Matthews hit the floor with a groan. Joe kicked the scalpel into a far corner.

"Are you all right, Nancy?" Frank asked.

Nancy nodded and brushed the hair from her face. Grinning at Frank, she said, "Just fine."

"Call the police, Joe." Matthews was coming around. Grabbing the doctor's shirtfront, Frank lifted him off the floor and snapped, "I've got a few more questions for you, Matthews. *Why* did you poison Glen Hewitt?"

"What?" Matthews asked groggily. His astonishment seemed genuine. "I never—"

"He was digging into the Valverde case," Frank said relentlessly. "You knew about his allergy. You had access to penicillin. You dropped in that afternoon and poured some in his coffee, right?"

"That's insane! I'd never—!"

"Sure! Just like you didn't try to run Ragnar off the road in that van," said Joe, getting off the telephone. "Where'd you go Wednesday morning, Doc? You sure weren't at the country club playing golf."

"Of course not! I changed my mind and decided to play tennis in Summerland." He trembled all over as the Hardys helped him up. "What are you people trying to do to me?"

"You gave Juan Valverde those steroids," Nancy accused. "And they killed him!"

"Now, wait a minute!" Dr. Matthews cried, his forehead sweating. "Yes, I gave Juan those Dynazol capsules. But it was at his insistence. I told him he didn't need them for a marathon. But Juan was desperate. He said there was some sort of well-paying contract at stake. He felt he had to outperform Gillespie. So I gave in and let him have that prescription."

"So it *was* the Dynazol that triggered Juan's heart attack," Nancy said. "You covered up and let Dave Gillespie take the blame for it."

"Yes." The doctor's reply was hoarse. "I couldn't afford to let the police find the Dynazol. The finger of suspicion would have pointed straight at me. I would have lost my license—my practice—*everything!"*

Then something Matthews had said clicked. "Well-paying contract." She remembered Tracy Reynolds's words. "Juan already had a big offer to promote sportswear."

Nancy couldn't shake Tracy's answers from her mind. And Tracy had ampicillin on her dresser! Ampicillin was a form of penicillin!

Matthews was on his feet now. His gaze was desperate. "I d-didn't try to kill anyone," he stammered. "You have to believe me!"

"Better save it for the judge, Doc," Joe said, hustling him out the door.

"I guess that about wraps up this case," Frank remarked, leading Nancy out of Matthews's office.

Nancy frowned. She wasn't quite so sure. She thought of Hewitt's poisoned coffee and those ampicillin capsules in Tracy's dorm room. She took Frank and Joe aside and told them her suspicions.

"You're right, Nancy," Frank said when she was finished. "Maybe I jumped the gun. Until they prove that Matthews tried to kill Hewitt, Tracy Reynolds is still a suspect. Let's keep an eye on her."

That evening the Hardys, Nancy, Ned, George, and Bess were the dinner guests of the Larsens and a few of their best friends and competitors. The news of Dr. Matthews's arrest was the chief topic of discussion.

Stuck at the head table, Nancy flashed Ned a conciliatory smile. But Ned avoided her gaze through all of dinner.

After dessert Dave stood and tapped a silver spoon against his empty water goblet. "Fellow athletes," Dave said, "I would like to propose a toast to our three talented gumshoes—Nancy, Joe, and Frank and their assistants." He reached for his glass of fruit juice. "Plus my personal thanks"—his face became solemn—"for finding out what really happened to poor Juan."

Glasses clinked around the table.

"And you even suspected me!" Lino touched his chest in mock indignation. "I ask you—is *this* the face of a *killer?"*

"A lady-killer, definitely!" Rosalia threw a crumpled-up napkin at him.

"Now we can concentrate on the Games, right?" Kurt smiled at them all.

"Right! I don't need Ridder's help to win," Lino said with a grin. "I can beat you all by myself, Larsen."

Ragnar laughed out loud. "Keep dreaming, Passano. Tomorrow I'm going to bury you."

"Let's call it a night, everyone," Dave added. "We've got five—no, six—big events ahead of us tomorrow. May the best man—"

"Win!" they all cried in unison.

Nancy tried to catch Ned's eye again, but he kept looking away. She was desperate to speak to him and explain about that scene at the beach.

Nancy saw Ned waiting at the exit. But before she could reach him, Sigrid had grabbed her. "I just wanted to thank you again, Nancy." The Norwegian girl looked relaxed for the first time.

"You're welcome, Sigrid," Nancy said, trying to keep an eye on Ned.

"There's still one thing I don't understand, though. Why was Dr. Matthews after me and Ragnar?"

Nancy looked at her curiously. That's a very good question, she thought. "I'm not sure about that myself," she told Sigrid.

Nancy fired a quick glance at the doorway, to see if Ned was still waiting. Her heart fell in her chest. He was gone!

"Is something the matter?" Concern shone in Sigrid's blue eyes.

Forcing a smile, Nancy shook her head. "It's nothing, Sigrid. I'll see you back at the dorm."

Nancy tried to ignore the heartache deep inside. Why are you so upset? she chided herself. You've got to see Ned tomorrow. You can make up with him then—she hoped.

After midnight Nancy was still awake, staring at the darkened ceiling. The sound of an occasional car passing hummed in her ears and combined with the muffled, gentle breathing of Bess and George.

Get to sleep, Drew, she told herself. The case is solved. Matthews set Dave Gillespie up as a patsy, knowing that any investigation would turn up the Valverde case and make Dave look even guiltier.

Nancy tossed and turned. No good. Frowning, she thumped the pillow a few times.

Annoying questions drifted out of the darkness.

For one thing Glen Hewitt hadn't gone looking for other suspects in the Valverde case. He thought Dave was guilty. He hadn't copied any old news stories dealing with Juan's death. Just that article on steroids. Why?

Of all the people she suspected of being Ridder, Dr. Matthews was the only one who *wasn't* at the refreshment table that morning. He wasn't at the beach the day Ragnar was cut, and he wasn't an expert javelin thrower.

Nancy's thoughts kept drifting back to that javelin.

Kurt Schweigert was an expert thrower. Of all the competitors, he had the strongest motive for wanting to beat Ragnar. Winning the decathlon would restore his overall athletic standing.

Unable to sleep, Nancy remembered the ampicillin capsules in Tracy's room. Powdered penicillin in capsule form. Tracy could easily have visited Hewitt and poured the white powder into his drink. The Ridder hoax could simply be an elaborate ruse to frame her old boyfriend Dave.

Sighing, Nancy dug her penlight out of her purse, flicked it on, and nestled it at her shoulder. She took out the copies of those news stories and reread the accounts of Juan's death.

Nancy's eyes kept returning to that photo of the funeral procession. Sad familiar faces frozen in time: Kurt, Lino, Jeff, Dave, Tracy, Grete, and Rosalia.

The somber faces of Grete and Rosalia were surrounded by displays of memorial wreaths. One had a ribbon whose letters were too small to read.

Taking out her pocket magnifying glass, Nancy could read its gilded message: Rest In Peace—Zip Sportswear.

Restless thoughts stirred Nancy's memory. Zip Sportswear—where had she heard that before?

Nancy flicked off her penlight. This was no good. She needed to rest because this case was by no means over. There were too many loose ends.

Finally, Nancy drifted off to sleep.

She dreamed of Padre Island. Frank, Joe, Ned, Bess, and George. Sunshine beating down on white-sand beaches. The rumble of motorboat engines. A pistol lifting ominously. The sudden blast of the gunshot, followed by the metallic ping of the ricochet.

That distant ping went on forever, its sound dragging Nancy into consciousness. All at once, the metallic noise seemed sharper. Nancy's dream noises faded, replaced by those of the real world.

Pungent diesel fumes crept into her nose and banished all traces of sleepiness. The air was thick and cloying. Rolling out of bed, she made her way to Bess and shook her awake.

"Nancy, what—" Bess blinked sleepy eyes.

Shaking George's shoulder, Nancy coughed. "Bess, get out!" she croaked. "The room's filling with fumes!" She pulled a groggy George to her feet. "Come on! Hurry!"

"Nancy, I can't see—" George began coughing uncontrollably.

"On your knees," Nancy gasped, pulling both cousins down. "Smoke rises. If you stay down, you'll be able to breathe."

They crawled toward the door. Nancy grabbed for the knob, turning it with a jerk. The knob broke off in her hand!

"What's wrong, Nan?" George choked.

Nancy cast a frightened glance at Bess and George and showed them the knob.

Bess let out a wail. "We're trapped!"

Chapter Twenty-One

NANCY POUNDED ON THE DOOR with her fist. "It's locked!" she cried. "It won't budge!"

"What are we going to do?" Bess asked frantically.

George tried to say something but succumbed to a coughing fit. Thick diesel fumes made the air unbreathable.

"Stay here!" Nancy cried.

Crossing the room, Nancy grabbed a pillow from each bed. Then, crouching beside her friends, she peeled off the pillow cases.

"Cover your mouths with these." Nancy balled one up and held it like a gas mask. "Stay close to the floor and follow me."

Nancy crawled on her hands and legs across the carpet. George and Bess followed.

We've got to reach the windows, Nancy thought groggily. Red spots danced before her eyes, and her lungs ached.

Looking back, Nancy spied Bess facedown on the carpet, not moving.

"George—" Nancy managed in a weak voice and nodded at Bess.

As George turned back for her unconscious cousin, Nancy held her breath, rose unsteadily to her feet, and shoved the window up all the way.

Fresh night air massaged her face. She felt strangely light-headed. She expelled her breath in one last frantic cry. "Help us! We're choking! Help!"

Then the green carpet swam before her eyes. That was the last thing Nancy remembered.

Sounds crept into Nancy's consciousness. Wood splintering. Shouting male voices. The distant howl of a siren.

Somewhere in the blackness she heard the familiar voices of the Hardys.

"What happened?" Joe was crying.

"The room's full of fumes." Frank's voice was tight with worry. "Somebody jam that air-conditioning vent!"

Frank and Joe, she thought, her anxiety subsiding. They came through again. . . .

A solid male hand closed around hers. Sighing thankfully, she murmured, "Frank—"

Then her eyes fluttered open, and Nancy looked into the stricken face of Ned Nickerson!

There was no mistaking the look of betrayal on Ned's face. Nancy felt as if her stomach had turned to ice. She realized at once how much that one word had hurt him. But having said it, there was no taking it back!

Ned concealed whatever he was feeling. "Are you all right, Nancy?" Genuine concern filled his voice.

Nancy felt like crying. Instead the fumes made her cough. "I think so. I just need some fresh air." She watched as Frank and Joe lifted a limp and senseless George and carried her out of the room. "How are they?"

"They're coming around," Frank said to Nancy, who followed them into another room, where Frank set George down on a bed.

"You lucked out this time, Nancy," said Joe. "If it hadn't been for Ned . . ."

Nancy reached over to give his hand a tender squeeze. "So you're the one who saved me."

Taking her hand, Ned smiled softly. "I couldn't sleep. I went for a drive. When I stopped in front of the dorm, I heard you screaming."

"Frank and I saw Ned running into the

dorm," Joe added. "We knew something was up, so we followed him. I pulled the fire alarm on my way upstairs."

Nancy could easily guess the reason for Ned's not being able to sleep. He must have been thinking about her and Frank Hardy, wondering if he'd lost her for good.

Nancy knew she couldn't put it off any longer. She had to tell Ned how much he meant to her.

"Ned, you and I have to—"

Nancy was interrupted by firefighters marching down the hall. While the Hardys explained the situation to the deputy fire chief, a paramedic came over and examined Nancy.

"She looks all right," the paramedic told Ned. "But I think all three of them ought to be checked for smoke inhalation."

Helping Bess sit up, the housing coordinator said, "You heard the man, girls. Let's go."

Anxious, Nancy blurted out, "Ned—"

Smiling a little, he helped Nancy to her feet. "I'll take you downstairs. Easy now. Lean on me."

Looking into his eyes as she took Ned's arm, Nancy felt one hundred percent better.

Frank and Joe made their way down the fire stairs toward the basement. Behind a gray metal door Frank heard the *chum-chum-chum* of a heavy-duty air compressor.

Joe gripped the steel railing for support and kicked the door wide open. He went through in a headfirst dive and came to his feet in a quick judo roll.

The basement was deserted. Joe flashed an all-clear signal.

Frank sighed in exasperation. "What have I told you about grandstanding?"

"Hey, what can I say? I've got *style.*"

"You'd think it was funny if someone was crouched behind that boiler with a gun!"

"You're paranoid, Frank."

Joe knelt beside the compressor. Thick, oily rags clotted the exhaust vent, forcing the diesel fumes to travel upstairs. Standing, he brushed the dust off his pants. "Frank, check to see if there's a control box around."

"Found it!" Frank opened a wall-mounted circuit board. "Very clever! Ridder stopped up that exhaust vent, then closed every room vent but Nancy's, pumping all the exhaust up there."

Joe shivered in disgust. "Good thing Nancy woke up."

"Well, he's long gone by now," Frank said. "Let's get back upstairs. I want a closer look at Nancy's door."

Five minutes later the Hardys were crouched in front of Nancy's door. The room itself still stank of diesel fumes.

After removing the outer doorknob, Frank

closely studied the lock mechanism. "Hmm . . . Ridder didn't leave anything to chance. After rigging the vents, he came up here and dismantled the doorknob. Then pushed the tumbler into the locked position."

"Good thing Ned was around." Joe lifted the stainless steel doorknob.

"Wait a minute!" Frank shouted. "We keep saying Ridder did this. But that means he's not Dr. Matthews!" He absentmindedly held the knob in his hand.

"Frank . . ." Joe wet his lips worriedly. "If it's not Dr. Matthews, then who is it?"

"That's what you, me, and Nancy are going to find out." Frank stood up. "We're right back to square one, and there's no shortage of suspects. Only it's a lot worse this time."

"How could it be worse?"

Frank's glance was deadly serious. "He didn't go after the Larsens this time. He went after Nancy! Ridder may be trying to get rid of us—*before* he kills the Larsens!"

"You'd better get some sleep," Ned advised, smiling down at Nancy.

She glanced at Bess and George, who were slumbering in a pair of twin beds. Following their checkup at the infirmary, the housing coordinator had moved them to a vacant room on the fourth floor.

"We really need to talk, Ned," Nancy murmured, leaning against her pillow. "I'm not sure you understand—"

"Shhhh! Tomorrow." Ned put his index finger to her lips. "I think I know what you're trying to say. And it can wait. For now, just get some sleep, okay?"

Nancy smiled softly. "You talked me into it, Nickerson."

Ned planted a feather-soft kiss on Nancy's mouth. Then, waving goodbye, he walked out of the room.

Tossing the bedcovers aside, Nancy rose and shut off the overhead light. As she turned, she caught a glimpse of the campus through the window. The stadium dominated the skyline, its upper rim illuminated with floodlights. The lights washed over a pair of billboards. One showed a pretty girl in a fleece jogging suit bearing the stylish legend, "Zip Sportswear"!

Nancy wandered over to the windowsill. She stared at the billboard curiously, conscious of a growing excitement.

Of course! Nancy thought, snapping her fingers. Now I remember. Zip Sportswear is the Games' sponsor. Mr. Overton mentioned that at the banquet. But why did they send that wreath to Juan Valverde's funeral?

Thinking back, another piece of the puzzle fell into place. Nancy remembered that *both* Tracy Reynolds and Dr. Matthews had mentioned something about Juan signing a contract.

Could it have been a contract with Zip Sportswear?

Nancy also remembered how Tracy had shut up right after mentioning it. Why had Tracy shut up? Was she under contract to Zip, too?

Then Nancy's eyes went wide. A realization came to her like a blinding flash. There was someone else, someone besides Tracy and Juan who was involved with Zip Sportswear. And that person was right here in charge of the Games, working directly with the sponsors. Jim Overton!

Chapter
Twenty-Two

"NANCY!"

Over the din in the stadium, Nancy heard Frank Hardy calling her name.

"Over here!" She saw the Hardys waving their arms over by the stadium's scoreboard. Athletes were lining up for the 400-meter run. The crowd was going wild.

She ran through bystanders, practically knocking some of them over. "Frank, Joe," she cried, trying to catch her breath. "You're not going to believe this, but last night I think I figured out why Ridder's after the Larsens."

"Last night?" Frank asked in amazement. "Why didn't you come and find us?"

Nancy shook her head. "It was late. Besides, that's not important. I'll tell you what is." With that, Nancy pointed to the giant Zip Sportswear billboard. "There's your explanation."

Joe looked at the billboard in confusion. "You're going to have to explain this one, Drew."

"Two years ago, Zip Sportswear was grooming Juan Valverde as an international contender," Nancy explained. "Tracy and Dr. Matthews told me that Juan had some sort of contract. It was very important to him. Important enough to risk his life to beat Dave Gillespie."

"What does that have to do with the Larsens?" Joe asked, confused.

"It's exactly what I suspected," Nancy said quickly. "Tracy Reynolds is the missing link, but not for the same reasons we thought. Yesterday, when Tracy told me why she'd never stoop to harassing Sigrid from leaving the competition, she called herself a professional. Now, why would an amateur athlete use that word?"

"If Zip had also made her an offer," Frank said slowly.

"Exactly." Nancy went on, "Sigrid is Tracy's big rival. Ridder's working for Zip Sportswear. He's protecting their investment by making sure that Tracy wins."

"I get it," Joe said, a wave of comprehension passing over his face. "The Ridder tricks were designed to frighten Sigrid out of the Games."

Frank ran his hands through his hair. "But that still doesn't explain who the mysterious Ridder is."

Nancy gave the Hardys a long, hard look. "Think! Who's representing Zip Sportswear here at the Games?"

"And who, as Games organizer, is able to go anywhere on campus and not be challenged?" Frank asked himself, following Nancy's logic.

"Wait a minute," Joe said. "I don't follow. You're saying it isn't an athlete?"

"Now you've got it," Frank said, smiling.

"Not Jim Overton! You know, if you two eager beavers had shut up for a minute, I would've come up with it."

"Nobody's keeping score, Joe," Frank replied. "Listen, we'd better find Overton—and fast! The women's fifty-meter freestyle is this afternoon. If Overton's going to move against Sigrid, he has to do it before then."

Joe's face went grim. "You're right. The only way for Overton to be sure she won't win a gold medal is to kill her."

"You guys find Sigrid. I told Bess and George I'd meet them. They were worried enough when I hurried off this morning. If I don't catch up with them, they'll wonder where I am."

"Okay, but be careful. Overton's out there somewhere."

Nancy nodded and waved goodbye. She scanned the field before heading for the stands. While maintenance men set up for the decathlon's final events, high school drum-and-bugle corps put on a show in the middle of the field.

"I don't believe my luck," Nancy said to herself. Standing over by the U.S. team was Tracy Reynolds. She was chatting with the female track and field athletes. Tracy must have seen Nancy coming, because she started to walk away.

"Hey, Tracy, wait up!" she shouted, running over to her.

"What is it?" Tracy asked sharply.

"I wanted to talk to you for a minute." Nancy wasn't going to let herself be intimidated by the girl. Not now. There was still a lot she had to know.

Tracy must have sensed Nancy's determination. She tossed her ponytail and nodded at the bleachers. "Can we make it private?"

"If that's the way you want it."

Nancy followed the girl off the field. Ducking under the bleachers, she trailed Tracy into the shadows.

Tracy turned abruptly, hands in her pockets. "What do you want?"

"You weren't completely honest with me

yesterday. You forgot to mention that Juan had a contract with Zip Sportswear."

Tracy's eyes widened in alarm. Nancy realized that her guess had been right.

"Dave Gillespie wouldn't buy into that Zip deal," Nancy went on. "He realized it would jeopardize his amateur standing. But you took Zip's money and promised to endorse their products after you secured a reputation. A win here at the Games would really pay off for Zip and you. You and your friend Ridder tried to kill Mr. Hewitt because he had everything."

Tracy burst into tears. "I had nothing to do with that. Honest! I *didn't!* Okay, I did sign with Zip, the same as Juan. They offered us a provisional contract. If we could win gold at a lot of smaller games and at the Olympics, Zip was going to use us in all their advertising campaigns. They wanted me to be the spokeswoman for a new line of swimwear."

"When did Hewitt come to see you?" asked Nancy.

"Just before the Games started. He asked me a lot of questions about Juan. He wanted to know why Juan had raced Dave."

"Did you tell him about the contract?"

"Not exactly." Tracy wiped her eyes. "But he was looking at me so suspiciously that I think he knew."

Nancy nodded in understanding. So Hewitt *had* changed his mind about Dave. The ex-cop must have wondered if Juan had given himself those steroids. After talking to Tracy, Hewitt must have put two and two together and come up with the reason behind Juan's desperate bid to win.

"I wasn't supposed to talk about the contract with anybody," Tracy added, sniffling. "After Mr. Hewitt left, I told my contact about the visit." Sobbing, she said, "I never wanted his help. Honest! I didn't even know what he was doing. I'd never hurt Ragnar or Sigrid. I'm not like that! I've always wanted to play fair and square. Nancy, I'm not a cheat!"

"No, you're not. But *Jim Overton* told you to keep your mouth shut and let him handle things. He threatened to ruin you unless you cooperated." Tracy was silent. "I'm right, aren't I?" Nancy asked quietly.

Tracy uttered a breathless sob. "Oh, Nancy, I'm sorry I ever got mixed up in this. Mr. Overton contacted me and Juan when we were still in high school. I never wanted any trouble. All I wanted was to be a championship swimmer."

Now it all makes sense, Nancy thought. Tracy told Overton about Hewitt's visit. Overton knew Hewitt would never rest until he had solved the Juan Valverde case. Once Hewitt had put it all together, including those Zip contracts, Overton decided to kill him.

Tracy was as much Ridder's pawn as any of

those chess pieces, Nancy realized. She put a hand on the weeping girl's shoulder. "You had no idea what was going on, did you?"

"No. Honest." Tracy wiped tearstained cheeks with her jacket sleeve. "I guess now I have to drop out of the Games, huh?"

Nancy sighed deeply. "I don't know." She touched the girl's chin and smiled a little. "If I were you, Tracy, I'd go right to the committee and tell them everything. Be honest with them, Tracy. It'll all work out for the best." Nancy's smile broadened.

"Thank you." Tracy smiled in spite of her tears. Then, head bowed, she zipped up her jacket and walked away.

Nancy took a step to follow her out. A sudden metallic click froze her in position.

She heard a sinister chuckle to her left. "You're all heart, aren't you, Nancy?"

Jim Overton stepped out from behind a concrete pillar, an oily black automatic nestled in his right hand.

"Back up!" he ordered.

Nancy did as she was told, stopping only when a metal upright piece touched her shoulder blades.

"Hands up! That's a good girl." He kept her covered. The crowd's roar doubled in volume. With a wry smile, he tilted his head toward the field. "Hear that? That noise will drown out any cries for help, you know. And any gunshots."

"How did you know we were down here?" asked Nancy, keeping her hands up.

Overton's evil smile widened. "You can see a lot from the broadcasters' booth. It was the only way I could keep track of you and the Hardys." He brandished the pistol. "Now maybe you can satisfy my curiosity. How did you figure out it was me? Did Tracy talk?"

"A lot of little clues kept pointing your way, Mr. Overton."

"Like what?"

Playing for time, Nancy said, "I saw you check out the hurdles before the steeplechase. You had to make certain that no one had discovered your sabotage job."

"Very observant of you."

"Two things gave you away, though." Anxiety made Nancy's knees shiver. "One was that little message you left in Sigrid's gym bag. That note reading, 'Pawns can't save you, Princess.' That had me stumped for quite a while. Then, after last night, it made perfect sense. Sigrid was the white queen. Frank, Joe, and I were the pawns. Ridder was taunting Sigrid, telling her that her detective friends couldn't protect her. All of which raised an interesting question: How did Ridder find out that we were detectives?"

Overton's eyes narrowed.

"You overplayed your hand that time," Nancy said. "Of all the suspects, only Dave Gillespie guessed that I was a detective. No one else found out until last night. Sigrid got that message *before* Dave guessed the truth about me. Therefore, Ridder had to be one of three people. The only people who knew about our undercover work were Dr. Matthews, Mr. Hewitt, and you!"

Jabbing the gun at Nancy, Overton snarled, "What else, Ms. Drew? I'm curious. Keep your hands high!"

"That stunt with the javelin," Nancy replied. "You thought you were safe on that one. Grete Nordstrom was a champion in javelin. Tossing that javelin at Ragnar pointed the finger of suspicion straight at Grete. Later on, though, I realized that Ridder wasn't really trying to kill the Larsens. Someone with fantastic aim and control had put that javelin right on the mark. That was no problem for the man who beat the magic three hundred!"

Sheer rage crept over his face. Overton's trigger finger tightened. "I ought to finish you right now!"

Nancy looked around desperately. She realized that her only hope was to continue stalling him. "That toss was *too* good. It was your best throw ever, wasn't it? An old jock like you just couldn't resist showing off." Nancy smiled grimly. "You shouldn't show off while committing a crime, Mr. Overton. It's like signing your name to it."

"Don't worry, Nancy. I'll keep it simple this time—just one bullet." Overton lifted the pistol menacingly. "You and the Hardys messed up the best deal of my life. Tracy Reynolds was perfect for the part of the Zip Sportswear girl. I spent thirty grand of my own money grooming her for these Games. All she had to do was win the gold medal, and I would have collected half a million dollars!"

"Plus whatever else you could blackmail out of her!" Nancy snapped.

Overton's eyes gleamed with a wild light. "It was perfect, Drew. A series of perfect crimes! Then you and the Hardys came along and ruined *everything!*"

His snarling voice sent chills through Nancy. The strain of committing these crimes had changed Overton. No longer was he the cool, calm master criminal. Before Nancy's eyes, he was changing into a crazed killer.

The crowd's roar rose to a pitch. Overton listened carefully. Then, flashing a bestial smile, he took dead aim between Nancy's eyes.

"Almost time for the fifteen-hundred-meter run." He chuckled. "Listen for the opening gun. It's the last sound you'll ever hear."

"No accident this time?"

Nancy's eyes flickered upwards. The two-by-fours of the bleacher structure were right over her head. They offered a very slim chance of survival. But still a chance . . .

"Oh, I don't have to be so elaborate with you," Overton teased, steadying his gun hand. "Nancy Drew, the famous girl sleuth. A lot of criminals would love to see you out of the way." He chuckled again. "The starter's gun will mask the sound of mine. One dead detective beneath the bleachers. An interesting problem for your friends, eh?"

Suddenly the crowd hushed. Nancy caught the last fragment of the announcement over the PA system.

"A fifteen-hundred-meter run! Gentlemen, take your places—"

Nancy inched her hands upward. Her fingertips touched a two-by-four.

The starter's voice drifted across the field. "Racers, take your marks—get set—"

She had gotten a grip on the beam, when she saw Overton's finger tighten on the trigger.

Horrified, Nancy watched as Overton drew back the gun's hammer and took aim!

Chapter Twenty-Three

LOOKING PAST Overton's shoulder, Nancy shouted, "Frank—no!"

Overton's eyes darted to the right.

Nancy jumped, her hands closing around the two-by-fours. She drew her knees to her chest in a single, fluid motion, then lashed out with a scissor kick.

Nancy's sole slammed into Overton's jaw, sending him sprawling. The gun went off. The bullet struck a nearby trash can with a sharp *ping*.

Dropping down, Nancy slid into Overton. Her foot caught and booted his gun hand. The pistol went clattering across the ground, coming to rest far under the stands. Nancy made a frantic grab for it. The pistol lay just out of reach. Seizing her by the ankles, Overton dragged her away from it. Rolling over, Nancy saw him towering over her.

Nancy twisted to the left, hooking the back of Overton's right ankle with her left instep. Then she delivered a sharp kick to his knee. Roaring in pain, Overton stumbled away.

"Nancy!"

Turning, she saw Frank and Joe running under the far end of the bleachers. Overton saw them, too, and fled, loping along with a stiff-legged stride.

"Don't let him get away!" Nancy cried, scrambling to her feet.

They pursued the fleeing criminal beneath the stadium's bleachers. Overton had a good lead, but every moment brought them closer. As they rushed onto the field, Nancy saw Overton heading straight for the security guard at the stadium gate.

Joe gasped. "What's he—?"

Frank's eyes widened in alarm. Cupping his hands, he shouted, "Guard! Stop him!"

The stadium crowd's excited clamor drowned out Frank's warning.

It was like watching a silent movie in slow motion, Nancy realized. Overton hobbled up to the guard. The guard looked puzzled. Overton pointed back at his pursuers. The guard stepped forward, unsnapping his holster. . . .

Then, in real time, Overton punched the guard from behind. As the man toppled, Overton slipped the revolver out of his holster.

"Get down!" Frank tackled Nancy, and they both hit the turf at the twenty-yard line.

Two shots rang out. The first bullet sizzled in the air above Frank and Nancy. The other splintered a bleacher post several inches from Joe.

Overton plunged through the gate, heading for the parking lot.

"Let's go," said Frank, hauling Nancy to her feet. "He can't run far on that leg."

"Be careful," Nancy warned. "He has four shots left."

"Terrific!" Joe muttered. "One for each of us, with one left over!"

Frank flattened himself against the stadium gateway's stone arch. "This time save the grandstanding, okay?"

Crouched in the shadows of the arch, Nancy peered beyond the stadium into the parking lot. There were thousands and thousands of cars, balloons and brightly colored pennants, and a popcorn stand. Overton limped across the asphalt, revolver in hand, looking around anxiously.

"We can't let him get to the end of the lot,"

Joe shouted. He broke from cover, racing toward the nearest line of cars.

Overton saw him and snapfired a round. Joe dove for a hardtop. The bullet starred the windshield of a green compact.

"Nancy—take the left," Frank hissed, launching himself to the right.

Nancy zigzagged along the stadium wall, then rolled forward behind the popcorn stand. Another shot from Overton's gun raised a puff of granite dust right next to her.

Only two shots left, Nancy thought. He'll be sure to make them count.

Hunched over, Nancy made her way through the rows of parked cars. From time to time, she peered over a hood, looking for Overton.

But there was no sign of him. Fine hairs bristled on the back of Nancy's neck. Her palms went cold.

He's ducked out of sight, she thought. He must have realized we were trying to outflank him. But which way did he go?

As silently as a ghost, Nancy tiptoed along the row. Suddenly Overton stepped out from behind the cab of a pickup. Seeing Nancy, he brought up the gun in a two-handed grip.

"Not so fast, Drew." Overton's eyes gleamed with malice. "I could use a hostage to get me out of here."

Nancy's eyes moved from side to side. Shiny new cars hemmed her in. But one of the cars had its windows rolled open.

Overton waggled a finger. "Walk toward me—real slow."

Nancy stood her ground. The open window beckoned. If only something would divert Overton's attention for a moment . . .

Suddenly Joe popped up behind a station wagon, both arms extended in a firing range stance. "Freeze! You're covered!" he shouted.

Whirling, Overton fired. Joe ducked behind the fender. The windshield exploded in a spray of safety glass.

Nancy dove through the open car window. Bouncing awkwardly on the back seat, she levered the other door open, rolled out of the car and crawled under the chassis.

Nancy saw Overton's legs by the car. "Where—" she heard him say.

Gripping the crankshaft for support, Nancy twisted her body around and swiftly kicked Overton's ankle.

She saw him go down as a shot rang out. His pistol went flying.

Nancy crawled out from under the car in time to see Frank vault the car's hood. He swatted the pistol aside, and, just as Overton was getting up, punched him in the jaw.

The Games organizer stumbled back, right

into Joe's reach. After spinning him around, Joe polished him off with a dynamite left hook.

Kneeling, Frank grabbed Overton's gun and thrust it into his belt. "Are you all right, Nancy?"

Nodding, Nancy climbed out from under the car. "I'm fine now." Standing, she shot Joe a puzzled look. "Thanks for the diversion, Joe. Where did you get that gun?"

"You mean this?" Grinning, Joe held up a plastic toy laser pistol. "In the back of the station wagon. I had one just like it when I was seven years old."

Frank groaned in exasperation. "Joe!"

"Hey, I told you I had style."

The following morning Nancy joined her friends in the dining hall for a celebration. Juice glasses were raised in toast to the exposure of Ridder and Dave Gillespie's victory in the decathlon.

"How did you do in overall points?" Joe asked Ragnar.

Holding George's hand, Ragnar grinned. "Pretty well. I was second."

"But you made me earn it, Ragnar. And I'm amazed you were even able to compete with everything that was going on."

"We'll meet again in the Olympics. And I won't have a bandage on my thigh."

Dave laughed merrily. "See you there!"

Bess glanced at Sigrid. "Does this go on all the time?"

Sigrid laughed, nodding. "Now you know what it's like living in a family of athletes." She aimed a thankful glance at Nancy and the Hardys. "If it hadn't been for you, Overton would have killed me for sure."

Ragnar put his glass down. "I'm glad the judges decided to let Tracy compete in the swim events."

George nodded. "Me, too. That was a brave thing she did, going to the Games committee after talking to Nancy."

Nancy looked up to see Ned entering the dining hall. Hurrying over to their table, he said, "Good news! I just got a call from Dr. Khatabi. Mr. Hewitt's going to be all right."

"That is good news!" added Frank.

"We should all stop by the hospital later on," Grete suggested, putting down her napkin.

"Good idea." Lino glanced idly at his wristwatch, then jumped from his chair. "Look at the time! We'd better get going!"

Glancing at the wall clock, Rosalia cried, "You're right."

"Excuse us, but we've got to change," said Dave apologetically.

Nancy turned to Ned and put her hand on his sleeve. Their talk was long overdue. She wasn't letting Ned get away this time.

"Before you get back to work, Ned, I want you to understand something. The other night, when I said Frank's name—"

Ned cupped her chin and smiled softly. "You don't have to explain anything. I understand what happened. Frank Hardy's a detective. I'm not. Naturally, you thought he was the one who'd rescued you." His smile turned rueful. "You and Frank work so well together—it's like you're practically one person. He's part of your detective life that sometimes takes you away from me. I think maybe I resent that a little."

Nancy opened her mouth to speak, but Ned beat her to it.

"Look, I can't change the way I feel any more than you can stop being a detective. Without that, you wouldn't be the Nancy Drew I know and love. If I want to be your guy, I'll just have to learn to accept it, that's all. And if you want to team up with the Hardys, be my guest. I don't mind—as long as I'm still number one with you, romantically speaking."

"Number one—now and always."

Nancy's eyes met his. Then, all at once, she was in Ned's arms, lifting her face to receive his kiss.

They were so lost in their kiss that they didn't even hear the chorus of "Ooooooohs!" that filled the dining room.

As Nancy and Ned broke it off, a ripple of

applause sounded. Ned's face went pink. Grabbing Nancy's hand, he murmured, "Maybe we'd better finish this outside."

An hour later Nancy and Ned stood in the midst of athletes inside the track. Looking toward the stairs, Nancy saw Frank and Joe heading for them.

"Where have you two been?" she asked. "For a while there, I thought you'd miss these events."

Frank smiled ruefully. "I'm afraid we are going to miss the rest, Nancy. We just got a call from Bayport. Another case."

"I know the feeling." Nancy returned his smile. "Till we meet again, Hardy."

Frank's smile broadened. "It's a small world, Drew."

They shook hands all around. As Nancy watched the Hardys saunter away, she wondered what kind of danger they would be facing. She knew they'd never ask, but maybe someday they'd need her.

"Help!" Bess wailed.

Clutching her team jacket and slacks, Bess rushed toward Nancy and Ned. George followed close behind.

"Bess, what's the matter?" Nancy asked.

Holding up her clothes, Bess made a woeful face. "Remember those exercises Dave taught me?"

Nancy nodded.

"My uniform doesn't fit anymore!" Bess flashed a look of horror. "I've been putting on weight faster than Dave's exercises could take it off!"

George sighed. "You had to have ice cream after every lunch and dinner, didn't you?"

"But I thought—" Bess wailed.

"Next time we're on a case together, Bess," she said with a smile, "remind me not to encourage you to get too involved!"